POSSESSED BY LIES

TRUTH OR LIES BOOK 5

ELLA MILES

Join Ella's Bellas FB group to grab my **FREE** book **Pretend I'm Yours**→Join Ella's Bellas Here

TRUTH OR LIES SERIES

Lured by Lies #0.5
Taken by Lies #1
Betrayed by Truths #2
Trapped by Lies #3
Stolen by Truths #4
Possessed by Lies #5
Consumed by Truths #6

PROLOGUE
ENZO

THE RAIN POURS all around me. The wind whips against my face. And my yacht rocks, high then low, as the water creates hurricane size swells.

But I grip the railing unmoving—nothing can push me anymore.

Not the sea.

Not the wind.

And sure as hell not the rain.

Because today, I lost everything, and no act of nature is going to be able to move me—I need revenge, for everything. For every loss, I need an equal act of vengeance. I need a loss for a loss.

But even that's not enough to bring back what I lost. Because I lost everything...

It started with my mother, and then continued, wiping out and affecting everyone I ever loved. I knew I shouldn't have let myself fall in love. I knew love would be the death of me, but I didn't realize it would also be the death of life as I knew it.

They ended me, so I will end them.

They think they will be ready for me. They will have their armies ready. Their weapons aimed at me. While I'm just one single man. I shouldn't be able to take down their entire army. I shouldn't be able to win.

But they can't kill a ghost. I've turned into nothing but a whisper of a shadow in the night. Barely a memory of the man I once was. There is nothing more they can take from me. And physical pain doesn't touch me, not anymore, not after what they did.

Mother.

Zeke.

Langston.

Liesel.

Kai.

All the people I loved—*gone.*

Why couldn't they take me instead?

My death should have been enough. It should have been enough to prevent all the people I loved from dying.

But they wanted me alive. They wanted me to live. They aren't finished with me yet.

But they will pay—for every single death. They kept the wrong person alive. If they had let Kai live, she might have been able to let my death go. She may have let them live.

I laugh. If they had killed me instead of Kai, she would have taken her time torturing every single one of them. It would have been worse off for them.

I don't plan on slowly torturing them, I plan on killing them all at once. Because I can't live with this pain. I need them gone. I need to get rid of this enormous ache in my chest, this emptiness in my belly, this loss of myself. *This loss of love.*

The wind lashes through me again, trying to thwart my plans.

My eyes turn red, and my heart stone—nothing will stop me now. Not until I wipe out every person who took my love from me.

I am unstoppable.

My heart has shattered. It no longer resides in my chest; it is scattered throughout my body embedded into every muscle, vein, and bone until all that is left of me is my heart. It encompasses everything I am. My bleeding heart is all that is left of me. I need to stop the bleeding. And the only way to do that is to kill them—all of them.

Blood for blood.

Death for death.

It's the only way.

And then I can let go. Then I can let the world consume me.

Somehow the wind picks up. Somehow the ship rocks harder. Somehow the rain pelts my face harder. And I don't know if mother nature is on my side, agreeing with my plan or trying to stop me. It makes no difference, because nothing can stop me, not anymore.

My body shudders, though, and the tears finally fall—hard, and I realize the sky is crying with me. Because my life isn't fair. My life is brutal. My life is gone. And I've had enough.

How do I live without everything that matters? The world may have thought by taking everything I loved it would turn me into the ruthless leader my father tried to develop. Instead, all that is left the empty cavity in my chest where my heart once resided.

I fall to my knees. *You win. You fucking win.*

The sobs continue, and the pain wrenches through my body like a continuous stream of nails plunging into my body. The pain will never stop again.

This is it—the end of my world.

And I'm more than ready for it to be over.

1

———

ENZO

"I love you, stingray," I say, my words traveling around the cabin of the yacht.

Liesel looks at me with a mix of yearning and sympathy, because she knows how Kai feels. She knows Kai won't say I love you back. Her feelings have changed. And our roles have reversed.

Liesel stands up from her chair, giving Kai a look that says we will talk more later. Then she walks toward where I stand in the doorway.

And I wish I would have entered earlier. I wish I would have heard Liesel and Kai's conversation. Liesel was the first one to get Kai to talk. It should have been me.

Instead, it was fucking Liesel.

And that kills me.

Liesel places her hand on my shoulder and gives me a squeeze. That gesture should comfort me. Instead, it breaks me further. Because her eyes tell a different story. Her eyes say, you have no chance. Kai has changed.

But I refuse to believe it. Kai has been broken before.

5

Kai has given up hope before. She's locked herself away before—this is no different.

I just need time to break down her walls again. Time to earn her forgiveness and trust.

Time.

I have plenty of it now that Milo is dead.

Liesel shuts the door behind me, and I stand with my hands in the pockets of my jeans. A gesture I've mastered ever since I got Kai back. With my hands stuck in my pockets, I'm less likely to reach out and touch her. But it still takes all of my willpower to not wrap her in my arms. To keep my lips from kissing hers tenderly, and passionately. I need to feel all of her. But that's selfish, and after failing her, I don't deserve to be selfish.

I take Liesel's empty seat across from where Kai is sitting as she stares out the large window of the cabin.

Kai looks at me as I sit, which I guess I should consider progress. She hasn't looked at me since the first night when I found her drenched in Milo's blood. Her body traumatized by what Milo had done to her. And that night, she begged me to fuck her. She wanted me to take Milo away. Rip him from her brain, and replace my body with his.

And I gladly gave Kai what she needed. I was hesitant, unsure if fucking her would help her heal or make things worse. But I did it. Because I needed the connection as much as she did.

And when we fucked, I thought we were going to make it. That it was the beginning of us healing from something so unthinkable. Something so painful and traumatic no person should ever have to suffer like that.

But the second my cum shot inside her, and she came down from her orgasm, everything changed.

Not like before—Kai didn't lock herself away with her

shield, her walls up to keep herself from hurting. This is different.

More happened than just Milo raping her. No matter how horrible that must have been for her, there is more. Because being raped would have been bearable for Kai. But whatever happened was worse.

I close my eyes and take a deep breath. I need to learn how to meditate or do yoga or some shit like that to keep my patience in check. I used to be so patient, so calm. I used to be able to handle any amount of waiting; delayed gratification was my middle name. But when it comes to Kai, I have no patience. I need her like I need air. And I need her to be happy and safe more than I need oxygen.

Truth or lie? I don't love Enzo Black.

Truth.

Those words slaughtered me. I've been through an eternity of pain over the last few months. My entire life, in fact, has been one long stream of torture. But those words killed me in a way I didn't think was possible. I felt suffocated. Still alive, but unable to get the breath I desperately needed. Just enough oxygen slipping through my lungs to keep me alive but in a state of pain forever.

It shouldn't hurt me. There was a time when I didn't think I was capable of love. And even when I realized I loved Kai, I never told her. I kept it to myself because I thought it was the only way to keep her safe.

How wrong I was.

In a way, it's only fair the second I decide to tell her I love her is when she no longer has feelings for me.

But when she loved me and I couldn't say it back, it didn't stop her from telling me any chance she got. And so I won't withhold my own feelings no matter how hard it is for me to say.

Because maybe, somewhere deep down inside, Kai does still love me. And I want that tiny seed to grow, until it spreads through her entire body again. Even if I don't deserve her love—because I failed.

"I love you, stingray. Even if you don't love me back. Even if you can never love me back, I love you."

She stares at me unblinking. Her lips don't even twitch to say anything back. This is a one-sided conversation.

No, Kai and I share a connection I've never experienced with any other person before. I don't need her words to understand her. I don't need her touch to feel her. I can feel her aura without needing touch or words. Just breathe her in.

But despite sitting so close to her, I don't feel anything—not anymore. I can't feel how fast her heart is beating. Unless I focus intently on her chest, I can't tell how quickly she is breathing. Her eyes are blank, giving nothing away behind her green eyes. Her body isn't drawn to me like it was before.

I can't read her at all.

"I'm sorry, Kai. You can't believe how incredibly sorry I am for letting Milo hurt you. I should have been stronger. I should have saved you sooner. I should have protected you. A better man would have." My voice cracks with each word. For the past month, I've been beating myself up about what I should have done. *I shouldn't have waited.*

I thought waiting was the right choice. I needed to regain her trust. I needed to show her she was in control of her own life. That I trusted her to make her own decisions. But I failed her in the process.

Milo might still be alive, but Kai would still be mine. I don't know how Milo accomplished it, but he held his promise. He took her from me. Kai no longer loves me.

She no longer breathes for me. She no longer longs for me.

It should have been me.

I should have been the one Milo broke, not Kai. But in the end, he chose her. And I think Milo knew he would never really become Black. That he would never rule. He was always destined to break Kai and me apart, even though he knew he wouldn't survive the betrayal himself.

I stare at Kai as the weight of what I let Milo do to her settles between us. My guilt has never been so strong. Not when I realized that Kai's father had sold her. Not when I made the same mistake myself and sold her to Milo, even though I saved her after. *This—this is my greatest regret.*

But this—I can't heal her if she won't let me in. Not even into the outer edges of herself. Not even into the bubble of her personal space.

I sigh when again Kai doesn't say anything nor react to my words.

"What do you need me to do, Kai? Tell me, and I'll do it. Write it down if you can't say it. Tell Liesel, and she'll pass along the message. I don't care what it is. If you need to punish me for what I did, then punish me. If you need me to push you slowly and gradually each day like I did before until you can talk and touch me again, then I will. If you need me to be patient and wait for you to come to me, I will. I can hire the best therapists in the world if that's what you need. If you are done with the stupid games we play for Black; I'll find a way to get you out of finishing. If you want to play our truth or lies game, I will. But I can't help you if you don't let me in. You don't have to say anything. Just give me a nod if I'm doing the right thing."

Nothing.

Blink.

Blink blink.

Blink blink blink.

That's her only movement—blinking. The only sign she is even alive. Her breathing is so weak I can't even see her chest rise and fall.

I lean forward in my chair with my hands in my lap, inching just the tiniest bit closer but not touching her. Not invading her space. But even the small inch closer makes my own heart beat rapidly and painfully in my chest. I'm so close, yet so far.

"This is killing me, Kai. You're the only thing in my world that matters anymore. I'm this close to giving Langston the power to run the empire, and running off with you to live on an island somewhere. As long as the people who depend on me are safe and taken care of. And Langston can do the job as well as you and I ever could."

Her blinking stops.

Yes! This is how she will communicate with me— through blinking. It's the tiniest of gestures, but when she first arrived in my house months ago so broken and beaten, she could only give the most minimal of gestures. This is no different.

All I needed was a drop of hope. *This is it—my hope.*

"You don't want Langston to become the leader?" I ask.

Her blinking speeds.

"Okay, Langston won't become the leader."

I pause, trying to figure out what is the most important things to ask without breaking her—without pushing her too far. But now that I have hope, I can't help myself.

"Do you blame me for what happened?"

Her blinking slows—no, she doesn't blame me.

I exhale a deep breath. She should blame me, but she

doesn't. I can live with that. *But then why will she talk to Liesel and not me?*

"You won't hurt me, you know? You may think you will hurt me if you tell me what Milo did to you. I understand if it is easier to talk to Liesel about what happened than to me, but I'm here. Whatever you need."

Her blinking remains steady, and I can't tell what it means.

I sigh, rubbing the back of my neck. My back aches from sitting hunched over in this too-small chair, but I don't care. I'd sit here all day as long as she gives me any sort of interaction, any amount of hope that we can heal from this.

"I want to touch you—hold your hand. Is that okay?"

I hold my breath as a lump in my throat grows, and the burning ache in my belly strengthens. After the last few weeks worrying about Kai, I'm surprised if I have any lining left in my stomach.

Steady blinking, but then, rapid—*her way of saying yes to me.*

I suck in more oxygen, not daring to let any of it leave because I'm not sure if this moment is real. Holding my breath is the only thing keeping me from throwing her over my shoulder and taking her away from everything. Because here we have to face reality, but away, we could start anew. A fresh start may be exactly what we need.

Slowly, I extend my right hand out toward Kai, hoping she will move the final inches toward my hand. I don't want to scare her or hurt her. I don't want to force her to do anything. I want her to come to me.

So I approach her like I would a stray dog. With caution, love, and patience. I hold out my hand and wait, but she never takes my hand.

I want to touch her.

And she said yes to me touching her.

But it still feels wrong when my hand grasps hers.

I can't let go, though. I need this to feel right. I need her hand to feel like it did before.

But when I look into Kai's eyes, I know. This is what she knew all along. This is why she wanted me to touch her. Not to feel hope that I can heal her, but to know in the depths of my soul that I can't. Kai doesn't want to be saved. She doesn't want to heal. She wants to live with her scars. And her scars won't let her love me.

I know the feeling. I've felt that way in the past. My father turned my heart sinister. He ensured that loving another would be the most difficult thing I ever did. So I fought with everything I had to prevent it. But still, I fell in love with the fiercest woman I've ever known. And it was all for nothing.

There is no hope left. *Can I keep fighting for us, when Kai has no hope?*

I stare down at our hands that have somehow intertwined with each other. *Did I do that? Or was it an automatic response from deep inside that forced our hands together in this way?*

My eyes drift up toward Kai's. They are still hollow, still empty. And I would give away all the love I feel for her just to give her back the soul in her eyes.

Fuck, I love her so much.

Love means never giving up. I can't as long as I love her. Kai may never be able to love me back, but it's not enough to stop me.

"Let go," she says, her voice full of pain.

I exhale all my breath and drop her hand. But I don't let go of her. I won't. *Ever.*

Kai Miller deserves the world. She deserves all I can give

her. All of the love I denied her for so long. I will never love again. Not like I love her. Our kind of love is rare and consuming.

Milo may have taken her love, but I still believe I can get it back. Somewhere deep down, her love is still there, hidden away. I just have to find it.

"Never," I say getting out of my chair and walking to the door, knowing I've pushed Kai far enough for today.

"I'll never stop loving you, stingray. There is nothing in this world that could stop me. I've denied myself loving you for too long—never again. Milo hurt you, I get that. But I'll never give up hope that you can find your way back to loving me. So that is the one request I'll never give you. I will keep fighting for you, forever."

———

TURNS out fighting for Kai is a lot harder than I thought it would be.

Kai tests me, every fucking day.

She tests me by not talking to me.

By not letting me touch her.

Feed her.

Clothe her.

Shelter her.

That one day was the only day she communicated with me. The only words she spoke to me. The only time her eyes spoke to me through blinking.

Now I get silence. If she even looks at me when I enter the room, I consider it a victory.

Most of the time she spends with me is locked away in her own head, or staring out at the ocean, reading a book, or watching TV. She's effectively shut me out.

It wouldn't worry me; I understand after what she went through with Milo she needs time and space to heal. She needs to feel safe and secure again. Her body has mostly physically healed, but the mind takes far longer.

So how long she is taking isn't my concern. My concern is that she is healing, just not with me.

Kai talks to Liesel—a lot.

Every single fucking day—for hours.

Liesel shares every meal with Kai. And then she will stay and talk for at least an hour or more. I've even over-heard them giggling together.

It stings. Every fucking giggle stings.

I love Kai's laugh. I love that she is smiling again.

But I hate that I'm not the one bringing the grin to her face. I'm not the one easing her pain away—Liesel is.

Since when did Kai begin to trust Liesel so much?

And each day their relationship continues, it gets harder and harder for me not to stand at the door and listen to every word they say.

I hear their whispered words, and it takes everything inside me not to rest my ear against the door. Or find the security tapes and watch every single conversation. Because I know Kai is telling Liesel the truth. Whatever happened that made Kai stop loving me, she tells Liesel.

And all I fucking want is the truth—and I'm about to get it.

I won't invade Kai's privacy; she would never forgive me for that. But I can make Liesel talk.

I pace in the hallway a few feet away from Kai's door. It's mid-afternoon. Liesel brought Kai lunch as always, and I know they are about to finish for the day. Liesel always heads to the pool by herself in the afternoon.

I torture myself by standing close enough to hear Kai's

voice, but far enough away I can only make out the occasional word.

Milo.

Rain.

The red one.

Pancakes.

Most of the words are trivial. I assume they are talking about the weather, clothes, and foods they want to eat. But I listen as they talk, knowing the conversation started with Milo. And I want to know more about what Milo did to Kai.

And then I hear the word that sends my heart into overdrive.

Enzo.

Fuck, what are they talking about?

The door finally opens, and Liesel steps out. She frowns when she sees me.

"What do you want?" she asks, crossing her arms as she stands in front of the door like a guard dog. "Kai doesn't want to see you."

"Then good thing I'm not here to see her. I'm here to see one of my bestest friends in the whole wide world who never keeps a secret from me. A woman who is smart, beautiful, sassy, and is a far better friend than Langston or Zeke ever were." *Please forgive me for lying, Zeke and Langston.*

Liesel rolls her eyes. "I'm not telling you anything."

"Liesel, I just need...something. Anything. I can't keep going on like this. I need to know how Kai is doing. What happened to her. How to help her. What she needs from me in order for us to start being us again."

Liesel bites her red lip. She looks worried, and Liesel never lets her worries show.

"Come with me," she says.

Yes! Yes, yes, yes!

She is going to tell me something, anything.

We walk upstairs to the main deck. She stops at the bar and pours us both a whiskey straight before sitting down on one of the lounge chairs.

I take a seat in the chair next to her, and my happy feeling quickly diminishes. She didn't bring me here to talk to me about Kai. At least not to spill any of her secrets.

"I'm worried about you," Liesel says.

"Why? I'm fine. It's not me you should be worried about."

"Kai is handling the break up just fine."

I growl. "We did not break up." Technically I don't even know if we were ever together. All I know is we aren't broken up. That seems far too final.

Liesel nurses her drink, while she waits for my blood to stop boiling. But she's going to be waiting a long time.

"Just tell me what Kai's hiding. Why is she able to talk to you and not me? What do I need to do to fix this?"

"Drink."

I frown. "Don't tell me what to do."

"I'm answering your question. You need to drink. You need to give her space. You need to continue on with your life. Take care of your employees and run the business."

"How the hell will that help me get Kai back?"

"It won't because you aren't getting Kai back. The Kai you knew is gone."

I stand up, as I toss my still full glass on the floor. It shatters instantly as whiskey stains the deck.

Liesel's eyes drop to the broken glass and then slowly flutter back up. She was expecting my outburst. She pauses a moment, then finishes her drink, before standing. Somehow we are eye to eye even though Liesel is over a foot shorter than me. Her heels and fury must make up the difference in height.

"I love you, Enzo. I would do anything for you. That's what love is. And I wish more than anything that I could stop loving you because the ache in my chest hurts all the fucking time. If I could just let go, I would. So I'm not going to tell you to let go, but I will tell you to move on. The pain won't get any better, but at least you will have a life. Something to live for instead of someone who doesn't love you back. I won't promise you that you will ever find that love in someone else. I haven't. And I can't promise you Kai will ever come back to you. She might, although where her mind and heart currently are, she won't."

I take a deep breath realizing as I stare down at Liesel's tear-stained eyes, how much she loves me, and how much I hurt her. I understand now more than ever. And it kills me to see her in so much pain.

"I'm sorry," I say.

"Don't be. Loving you and thinking you could love me back was one of the greatest highs of my life. Realizing you will never love me was one of the greatest lows. Accepting that there is nothing I can do about that love is what has helped me to survive in a way that allows me to not spend my life drinking a bottle of whiskey every night."

I nod. I understand, but her words don't help.

"Now, let's go get another drink. And then we can sit and talk about the people we love who will never love us back."

"But I thought you said to move on."

She sighs. "You weren't listening at all. I told you I would never tell you to move on; it's not possible. I said to keep living. And part of living is talking about the people we love. So tonight, that is what we will do. Tomorrow, you will try to go an hour without speaking her name. Thoughts of her will still be there, but you won't be allowed to speak them. Next week, you will try an entire evening. And then one day you'll learn to go days without speaking her name. And you'll realize that an entire hour has gone without her crossing your mind. That's when you'll realize she doesn't own you. That's when you'll realize she didn't take everything from you. She left one tiny piece, and that piece is what you will build the rest of your life around."

"Can't you just tell me what Kai's hiding? I think it would be a better use of my time to talk about how to win her back instead of talking about her in the past tense."

She shakes her head and grabs my hand. The touch feels nice since I haven't held Kai's hand in a while, but it's nothing like the spark I get from Kai.

She pours us both another drink and then hands me my glass. "Try not to break this one this time."

I take the glass reluctantly. Drinking myself into oblivion sounds nice, but I've tried that option. It always makes things worse in the morning. And it doesn't feel fair to Kai. Kai may be talking to Liesel, but that doesn't mean she's healed. It doesn't mean she's over whatever Milo did to her. So I'll have one drink, but not more.

I follow Liesel back out to the deck and take a seat next to her, slowly sipping on my whiskey.

"So you want us to talk about the people we love who don't love us back?" I ask.

She nods.

"You do realize the person you love who doesn't love you back is me, right?"

She moans and downs her drink. "I'll be right back with the bottle."

I laugh and take another long sip of the alcohol. It would be so easy to ease my pain with alcohol, but I won't.

Kai deserves a better man. And that's how I plan to live my life until I find a way back to Kai's love. By showing her how much better of a man I am. And how I'll spend my life showing her.

Five hours later, Liesel and I have talked ourselves out. Liesel is drunk after finishing the bottle mostly by herself. I did drink more than the one drink, but I've never felt so sober.

Liesel, on the other hand, won't even be able to stumble back to her cabin.

"Come on, I'll carry you," I say, throwing her arm over my shoulder and cradling her legs.

She smiles brightly up at me as her red fingernails touch my cheek.

"You like me," she says.

She's so drunk.

I nod. "Yes, Liesel, I like you. We are best friends, remember?"

She moans. "Ugh, friends."

I smile, she's going to regret this in the morning. She may have said we were both going to talk about the people we love, but I mostly talked about Kai while Liesel talked about all the men in her condo building she wants to get with and which of the Hemsworth brothers are the hottest.

"Are you sure? Because I think I feel something hard poking me in the ass?" she says.

I roll my eyes. "That's my phone in my pocket."

"Oh," she frowns.

I carry her down the hallway toward her cabin. Her room is a couple of doors down from Kai's. This yacht is nice, but not as nice as the *Savage*. It doesn't have any special security modifications on it to have separate areas. All the cabins are basically the same.

As I walk past Kai's room with Liesel still in my arms, I listen, and beg the door to open. I hate going to sleep at night without getting a glimpse of Kai.

But instead of a glimpse, I hear voices. She's not alone.

The other voice is male and belongs to one of my best friends—Langston.

I bite my lip hard. *What the hell?*

Liesel, even in her drunken state, notices my change and laughs. "You think Langston would fuck Kai?"

"No...maybe...I don't know."

Her laughs turn into uncontrollable giggles, then snorts.

"What's so funny?"

"You are silly." She touches my face again, but this time it's more like a scratch from her nail.

I exhale deeply, trying to calm the hell down. But I want to burst into Kai's bedroom and figure out what they are doing.

"They are sleeping together," Liesel says, answering my unspoken question.

"What?" I snap.

"Sleeping, to-geth-er," Liesel yawns as she breaks each syllable apart.

"I heard you. I thought you said they wouldn't fuck each other?"

More laughing until I can barely contain her in my arms.

I sigh, walk the extra couple of feet to Liesel's door, kick it open, and plop her ass on the bed.

"Start talking." I cross my arms over my aching chest. *Please have an innocent explanation.*

"They are sleeping together."

"Yea, I heard that part. Why? When? Explain."

Liesel snorts which only makes her giggle again. "You think I mean fucking."

"Liesel, I'm not playing games, what are Langston and Kai doing behind that door?"

"SLEEPING."

Finally, her words sink in. "Just sleeping?"

She nods hurriedly.

Thank fuck, I exhale.

"Since when?"

She shrugs. "The first night. Kai gets nightmares. She needs someone with her. She doesn't trust me, and I come to bed most nights drunk, but she trusts Langston."

I grin. Finally, I have some ammunition I can use. Something I can do to force us to spend some time together. Something I can understand about what happened.

I turn.

"But you can't! Don't tell her I told you! She won't be happy. We have an understanding—a truce."

"What sort of understanding?" I ask, maybe I should have gotten Liesel drunk earlier. She's answering a lot more questions now than she was earlier in the night. Even if I have to decipher what she means.

"I mean understanding." She gets on all fours on the bed and crooks her finger to come to me.

I walk to her and lean my ear down.

"We tell each other secrets."

"And what are those secrets?" I ask.

She shakes her head. "I mean, we keep each other's secrets." And then she snaps her hand over her mouth like she wasn't even supposed to say that.

"Get some sleep, Liesel." I walk out of her room and close the door. I've gotten all that I'm going to get out of her tonight.

But I got enough. Kai has nightmares. And Langston has been helping her.

Kai may not love me anymore, but she's going to accept my help.

I storm down the hallway and stop in front of her door. I resist the urge to barge in and instead knock three times. Then I wait. Because for the first time since I got Kai back, I have a plan to spend the night with her.

2

———

KAI

LANGSTON STANDS in the corner and removes his shirt revealing the leanest body I've ever seen. If I wasn't so fucked up, I'd be drooling right now. I'd be hot and bothered and trying to find a way to seduce him into my bed.

I already get Langston in my bed.

He's been sleeping in my bed every night, trying everything in his power to keep my nightmares away, but they always come back. We discovered being able to rest my head against his bare chest so I can hear his heartbeat against my face sometimes calms me down, hence why he's shirtless.

He climbs into bed, waiting for me. I remove my shirt, standing in a thin tank top and shorts. I prefer to sleep naked, but it bothers Langston. I'm completely secure in my nakedness. I have no problem with men looking at my body, but it's pushing too far for Langston and I's strictly platonic relationship.

I get into the bed and lean against his warm, hard chest, trying to heat up before I sleep. Langston's body is definitely warmer than mine, but it is nothing compared to Enzo's body.

Langston shivers at my touch.

"Sorry," I say, knowing my touch chills him.

"Don't apologize. I want to help, even if I become an ice cube after you touch me."

He's a good man. I used to think Zeke was the good one, but Langston's heart is just as big. And Enzo...I can't go there. Enzo is such a mix of good and bad. One moment he's killing innocent people, the next he's saving them. I'm the perfect example of how Enzo doesn't stand firmly on the good or bad side. He's saved me from death and sold me. He's hated me and loved me. I can't go back to that. I can't go back to not knowing whether he loves me or hates me, even if it seems his love is real this time. It's too late. His love isn't enough to overcome my own problems.

I try to match my breathing to Langston's slow, steady breaths, knowing that is the only way I will be able to get to sleep. But my stomach starts doing these weird flips, and I know what's about to happen. My morning sickness has been pretty inconsistent so far, but it's been happening more and more at night.

"Be right back," I say, jumping out of Langston's arms and running to the bathroom.

I feel queasy, sweaty, and weak gripping the toilet, waiting for the inevitable to happen.

I close my eyes and take long deep breaths as my stomach slowly quiets.

False alarm.

I sigh and lean against the wall.

"How far along are you?" Langston asks.

I jump. I didn't realize he had followed me into the bathroom.

"Um..." I try to stall as I get up off the floor and walk to the sink to rinse the acidy taste out of my mouth. The fewer people that know about the baby, the better. I shouldn't have even told Liesel, but I just needed to tell someone. *And if Langston knows, how am I going to keep it a secret from Enzo?*

Langston hands me a mint.

I take it and plop it into my mouth, the cooling flavor settling my stomach even more.

He cocks his head to the side and crosses his arms, waiting for me to answer.

"A few weeks. How did you know I'm pregnant?" I ask.

"I have an older sister who lived with me when she was pregnant while she and her husband were remodeling their house. I know the symptoms."

I'm surprised to hear Langston has a life outside of fighting alongside Enzo. It doesn't seem like it's possible.

"Does Enzo know?" he asks.

I slowly shake my head no.

"Why not?"

That's a loaded question with about a million answers. But there is one simple answer that encompasses all those reasons.

"Because I'm scared."

Langston's face drops as his arms go around me, and he pulls me hard into his bare chest. His heart thuds against my ear far too fast. He's scared too.

"I went from being desperate to have a child, to being terrified. How messed up is that?"

Langston's eyes grow wide as he lifts my chin so he can see my eyes better. "That would be normal for most women, but for you, a woman who is locked in a world filled with danger, it's expected."

He rubs my back gently as he begins to think about what this means.

"Is the baby..." he can't finish that sentence, but I know what he's asking.

"I don't know if the baby is Enzo's or Milo's, but it doesn't really matter."

He frowns. "Why doesn't it matter? I would think you would be thrilled if it were Enzo's."

I swallow hard. I should be thrilled. A few days ago, I was desperately in love with Enzo and would have done anything to be with him. Now, I don't know how I feel. Milo turned all my feelings for Enzo upside down. All I know is I don't love him. I know what it's like to love Enzo and these feelings aren't it.

"I don't love Enzo anymore."

Langston nods. "But I'm sure you'd still rather it be Enzo's than..."

Again he can't finish. "Than my rapist? Of course, I'd rather it be Enzo's, but..." *God, now I'm the one who can't finish my sentences.* "But my child is in danger no matter whose child it is. Either way, my child becomes an heir to the most dangerous organization in the world. This child will inherit untold riches, and have more money than they could ever spend. But they will also have enemies set on killing them from the day they are born. Others will try to use them as a pawn to gain their own power in the Black organization. I just want my child to be safe."

Langston runs his hand through his hair, and I swear I see moisture in his eyes. He knows this won't end well for me and my child, no matter what I do.

"So what are you going to do? If Archard finds out you are carrying a child, that child will become your heir. They won't have a choice but to fight in the games when the time comes."

I think of Liesel. She had a child, possibly Enzo's child. And she hid it. She had to give up the child, but he's safe because she protected him. I can do the same thing.

"I will hide my child, from everyone. No one will know I have an heir. I will hide them forever, even from Enzo."

"Are you sure you can do that? I know you don't love Enzo now, but you two share a lot of history. Are you going to be able to keep this from him? I've only spent a few nights with you and I figured it out. Enzo knows you better than anyone. Don't you think he'll be able to figure it out?" Langston strokes my cheeks as he speaks, rubbing the moisture off my face.

"That's why I can't stay. I need the games over. I need to get the hell out of here before he notices. Enzo and I have suffered enough; this game ends with us. Once Enzo becomes the ruler, he can change the rules to ensure his second in command will take over instead of his child. Or two people from within the organization can compete, but I'm not involving my flesh and blood in this."

Langston nods as he stares into my eyes. "What else aren't you saying?"

"If the child is Enzo's, you aren't going to try and kill him or her, are you?" my voice shakes. I hate that I'm even questioning Langston, but after what Milo said, I don't know who to trust. I need Langston to reassure me. If he lies, I'll be able to know.

"What? Why would I hurt your child? I don't care if the child is Enzo's or Milo's. I care about you, Kai. You deserve better than this world. Better than what Enzo, or Zeke, or I have done for you. I would protect your child with my life because it's yours, I don't give a shit who the father is because I know the child's mother is worthy."

"Truth," I sigh at his words. "You spoke the truth."

"Of course, I fucking told you the truth. What's going on?" Langston grabs my shoulders.

"I can't trust anyone within the organization with my secret. I shouldn't have even trusted you, although I'm glad someone else knows. But I can't trust anyone else. If they think the baby is Enzo's, they may try to kill him or her. The team wants the strongest. They want to see two people battle to become Black. If Enzo and I share an heir, then there won't be a fight to become the leader. Our child would become the ruler automatically. The men won't let that happen. They'd rather kill our child than let them lead. They will try to force us to both have heirs of our own. Ones who will fight each other when the time comes."

"That can't be true. If you had a child together, they would think that person would be the strongest. The best of both of you. They wouldn't try to kill your child. They trust and respect Enzo," Langston says.

"It's happened before. I can't trust that even a small segment of the crew might feel that way and lead a revolt to try to harm my child. I can't trust anyone. No one in the Black organization. No one outside of it. Not even Enzo."

"Are you sure? Enzo might be the only one who will be able to heal you. To fix you after the nightmare Milo caused you. I'm doing my best here, but you aren't getting any better. If anything, the nightmares are getting worse. He could heal you. He could help you."

"And what about the baby? Enzo hasn't been able to protect me, what makes you think he could protect our child?" It's a low blow, especially since I was the one who put myself in danger with Milo. Enzo was just respecting my choice. But it's the truth. I don't trust anyone but myself with the protection of my baby.

Langston is silent. He doesn't even try to answer because he knows it's the truth.

"I don't want Enzo to fix me. I can't fall back in love with him. I can't risk my child's life for selfish love."

"Then I will help make sure you don't fall in love again. And when the time is right, I will help you disappear from everyone, even from me. The only way you will be safe is if you vanish."

I see the pain in Langston's face. He is no longer Enzo's trusted soldier; he's mine. He will put me first, above Enzo. And if Enzo knew the truth, he'd want Langston to put me first. To protect me even from himself. I can see in Langston's eyes what the plan is, what is going to need to happen to protect me. And even though I don't love Enzo, my heart already breaks for him.

———

I HEAR THE KNOCK: three loud, determined pounds. Not meant to scare me, but enough to know who is standing on the other side of the door.

Enzo has mostly respected my privacy. He only ever comes into my room a few hours every day—usually in the afternoon. He doesn't push me. He doesn't force me to speak. To touch him. To interact at all. But something about that knock tells me he's past his patience.

Langston looks at me with weary eyes. He's not in the mood for a fight either.

"What do you want me to do?" he asks.

Langston has been sleeping in my bed almost every night these last few weeks. It shouldn't help. But I tried having Liesel sleep next to me, and the nightmares got worse.

I need a man to sleep next to me. One I trust. One I know can fight off Milo. One whose arms remind me of Enzo's.

Dammit. How is it even though I don't love Enzo anymore, I still lust after him? I still long to be in his arms? To feel his cock inside me? Couldn't Milo erase those feelings too if he was going to take away the love part? It would be easier. Because even though Enzo scares me, even though his touch now hurts me, my body still craves him deep down. It's the most confusing thing ever.

"Answer it," I say, knowing Enzo isn't going to leave.

Langston gets out of bed. And I realize our mistake as soon as the door opens.

Langston is shirtless except for his boxers. And I look naked in bed with the sheet pulled up to my chest.

We both sleep better without clothes on. And we've found that at night when I have the nightmares, the only thing that helps calm me and bring me back to reality is our skin touching—already being shirtless helps.

There is nothing sexual going on between us. It's more of a brother and sister relationship. But the way Enzo is looking at us says he sees something very different.

"What do you want? We are trying to sleep," Langston says.

Enzo growls. "What am I doing? What the fuck are you doing?" Enzo throws a punch before Langston can react.

I wince as his hand connects with Langston's jaw.

Langston immediately strikes Enzo back, hitting him in the eye.

Such boys.

"Stop it," I say.

Enzo's mouth goes slack as his punch stops mid-air. I've denied him my voice for so long that two simple words make him stop thinking about killing Langston for long enough to pay attention to me.

I sigh. I don't like seeing Enzo hurt, even if I don't love him. Even if a part of me hates him. And Langston sure as hell doesn't deserve to be injured.

"She doesn't want to talk to you, man. So get the hell out," Langston says, trying to protect me.

"No fucking way. You don't get to sleep naked with my woman."

"She's not your anything. She's her own woman. She can make her own decisions, and she doesn't want you here."

"I'll leave if she tells me to leave," Enzo says, turning to me. The ball is in my court.

I could easily tell him to leave, but for some reason, I don't want to. I'm physically exhausted. Last night was torture. I barely got any sleep between the night terrors and the morning sickness. Morning sickness my ass; mine likes to hit me in the middle of the night.

There is something drawing me back to Enzo. It's not love, more like curiosity. We have shared more together than I have with any other person. If anyone can keep the nightmares away, it's him.

And as for the morning sickness, this baby might be his. I don't logically think that him being near would stop the sickness. I know that's not how it works. But it's worth a shot.

So I don't say anything.

Enzo smiles.

Langston looks to me. "Do you want me to go or stay?"

I don't want to speak again, so I nod for him to go.

Langston nods back. "I'll be right outside if you need me."

"She won't. She needs me," Enzo says confidently, walking over to the bed.

Langston shuts the door on the way out, and I know he will keep to his word and sleep in the hallway all night. I never thought I'd need Langston to protect me from Enzo. And it's not that I need protection. I know Enzo won't physically hurt me. But it doesn't stop my body and mind from playing tricks on me.

"Why didn't you tell me, stingray? Why didn't you tell me you were having nightmares?"

I don't answer. *Because I don't want you to have any hope.*

He smiles. "Don't worry about me having hope. If you truly don't love me and can't love me again, then my hope is gone."

I narrow my eyes, not believing him.

He chuckles.

Why is he being so lighthearted about this?

"I'm going to guess the nightmares are about Milo?"

I nod almost involuntarily. They are about Milo, but also about someone else.

He grins again, as if he is winning a prize.

"And Langston hasn't been able to keep them away?"

I shake my head.

"It's because you had the right idea, but wrong man. Don't get me wrong, Langston is a great friend. Someone you should talk to, but I'm the only one who can help you with this. Our connection is too great, even if your heart disagrees."

He pulls his shirt off over his head and kicks his shoes off.

Damn.

I forgot how built he is. Every muscle appears sculpted into his body. There isn't an ounce of fat on him, and that damn V disappearing into his pants does things to my body I don't understand. Even his rough scars draw me in and make him more attractive, reminding me of how hard he fights to get what he wants. I shouldn't want someone so cruel.

I lick my lips.

He notices.

"I could always take care of other needs, too. It might help you sleep to be sated and spent. You'll sleep hard, dreaming of my cock instead of..." his voice trails off as he realizes his mistake.

Bringing up Milo.

Any sexual thoughts shut down.

For both of us.

Enzo doesn't speak again as he gets out of his pants and then into the bed next to me.

He turns the lamp off, and then we are in total darkness. He lays back on his side of the bed, giving me space.

"I love you, stingray. I will never stop loving you."

I close my eyes. *I wish you would stop.* Because every time you say those words, I feel a tinge in my heart as if it's reawakening a little. What I wouldn't have given to hear him say that before. But I ended up giving away all of myself in order to hear those precious words.

I sigh and grip the covers tighter to my body.

"I'm here if you need me," his voice hangs in the air.

But I don't speak back.

Enzo is here. And for the first time in weeks, I fall asleep within minutes. Even though I know my nightmares are going to be about him.

3
———

ENZO

I WATCH HER SLEEP. And I know I won't get one second of sleep tonight. Because I miss everything about her. And this is my only chance to soak all of her in.

Her smell.

Her breath.

Her aura.

But I still can't get the one thing I'm desperate for—her touch.

Or her words.

Or her love.

Those things she has locked away, and I need to know why. What happened so that she will no longer allow herself to feel anything but pain toward me?

Kai's breathing turns rapid and shallow instantly. I'm surprised she was able to fall asleep so quickly. She must be exhausted from how little sleep she's been getting with Langston trying to help her. Didn't she know I was the key all along to her getting more sleep?

Langston is a good man. He'd do everything he could to protect her. But he's not me. He doesn't love her like I do.

He's not as skilled as I am. And he doesn't have a rage growing inside him, blame for losing her again.

On second thought, maybe he is better capable of protecting her. Because I've failed so many fucking times. I don't even deserve to earn the title of Mr. Black. If I'm incapable of protecting Kai, then I'm incapable of protecting the men and women who work for Black.

"No..." Kai's bottom lip trembles as she says the word so softly I'm not sure she actually spoke.

I lean over on my right arm and scoot closer to her, but I don't touch her. I won't unless she wants me to. And since she can't give consent in her sleep, I'm in a bit of a jam.

Maybe it's not a nightmare, maybe it's just a simple dream.

But when she says 'no' again, her voice is deeper, stronger, more determined than before; I know who she's saying no to—Milo.

"Kai," I say, calmly, hoping it's enough to wake her up, or at least calm her brain enough to let the nightmare go.

"No, don't fucking touch me," Kai murmurs.

I sit up, moving as close as humanly possible to her without touching her. I run my hand through my hair in frustration.

"Kai!" I practically scream. I can't stand her in pain. I can't handle seeing her like this. "Wake up, baby."

"No, get off me, Milo," Kai says louder. Her face and hair are drenched in cold sweat, and her arms wrestle with the blanket wrapping around her.

I try to remove the blanket and sheet from her, but they are so tangled around her body there is nothing I can do without touching her.

Her face squeezes hard, as if experiencing pain. As if Milo is forcing himself inside her all over again.

Jesus Christ.

"Kai, wake up. I can't help you unless you tell me to. Wake up, stingray."

But Kai doesn't wake up, she tosses in the bed, fighting an invisible man who will always be present in her mind, terrorizing her dreams.

"No!" Kai screams again, her body jerking.

I can't stand it anymore; I have to do something. I have to make this stop.

I reach my hand over hers to pull her into my body, hoping her body will recognize mine and calm down.

"No, Enzo!" Kai screams.

Her eyes are still closed, and she seems to still be in the midst of a nightmare.

My hand floats over her body, but I don't dare touch her, not after her words.

I wait for more.

"Stop, don't touch me, Enzo."

My heart drops. I don't know what's happening, but her nightmares seem to be as much about me as they are about Milo.

"I'm going to help you, just hold on," I say, jumping out of the bed, and hating I have to leave her alone for even a second.

But I unlock the door and practically throw it off the hinges. And then I see Langston, pacing the hallway. I've never been happier that he disobeyed my orders.

Langston's face snaps to mine with an anger I've never seen on his face before.

"You did this to her. She doesn't want you anymore. Let her go," Langston says calmly. And then he brushes past me, our shoulders connecting in rough impact as he makes his way to Kai.

I follow him into the room, but keep my distance as Kai continues to alternate between screaming Milo and my name.

Langston doesn't hesitate to touch her. Apparently, she's already given him permission.

"Kai, you're safe. I have you. You can wake up," Langston says, wrapping her in his arms. Pulling her head to his bare chest to try to warm her and stop the cold sweats.

He slowly rocks her as he whispers more words into her ear I can't hear.

Slowly, Kai's eyes open. But she's still not here. She doesn't look at Langston. She doesn't look at me. She just stares as if she's still living her nightmare.

Langston begins stroking her hair and rubbing her back gently.

"You're safe. No one is going to hurt you. Never again," Langston says. Making promises I've made before, but was incapable of keeping.

Fuck.

What did I do? How could I have let this happen?

Suddenly, Kai jumps up and runs to the bathroom.

"What's happening?" I ask, Langston.

Langston sighs. "The nightmares are so real that sometimes she gets sick afterward."

I don't deserve her. And all I do is hurt her.

But I'm a selfish bastard. I fell in love. And I don't think I can let her go.

Langston and I both follow Kai to the bathroom, where she grips the toilet as she empties everything in her stomach. No wonder she looks so weak and doesn't want food, if this is what happens later at night.

Langston pulls her hair into a ponytail and rubs her

back. What I wouldn't give to be able to do that for her. But he gets to, not me.

I go over the sink, grab a washcloth, and wet it with warm water.

I close my eyes, wincing with each wretch of her stomach. Each time she vomits, I feel a direct hit to my core. I'm the one being hit.

Finally, the sound stops, and I turn to look at Kai. She's pale, looking like she just finished running a marathon.

This is my fault.

Langston is still standing behind her, waiting until she's ready to get up. But I don't deserve to get answers. I don't get to be here anymore.

I will help fix her, but not for my own selfish reasons. Because she deserves to be whole again. She deserves to go through life without living in pain.

I hold out the washcloth to her with a sadness and pain I haven't felt since she risked her life to go with Milo.

Langston reaches out to take it for her, but Kai beats him to it. When she grabs the washcloth, her fingers brush mine, and I'm overcome with her pain. That's all I feel when I touch her, and it's because she's so consumed by it that she can't feel anything else.

I feel the tears swelling in my eyes, and I know I can't stay. She doesn't deserve to have to deal with my tears. My pain is nothing compared to hers.

I turn and begin walking quickly out of the room, knowing I won't bother her again unless she asks me to. Which she never will. Which means this is effectively goodbye.

Damn fucking goodbyes.

"Stop," Kai says, her voice weak yet strong.

I stop but don't turn around as I force my eyes to suck the tears back into my eyes.

"Langston, will you go get me some water?" Kai says.

"Of course," Langston says and begins walking.

"Take your time," Kai tells him.

And then it's just her and me.

"Truth or lies," she starts.

And I slowly turn around, shocked she is talking to me after what she went through. She's still sitting on the floor in front of the toilet, as if she doesn't trust herself to not vomit again.

Kai's wearing panties and a thin tank top exposing her soft nipples to me. But I'm the one who feels naked in only my boxers. Not because of the clothes, but because of the way she's looking at me, like her words are about to destroy me, and make me vulnerable in a way I'm not ready for.

"I hate you for letting me get taken by Milo," she says.

I suck in a breath—*yep, I'm not ready for this.*

"Truth," I exhale.

"Lies, I don't hate you for letting me make my own decision. I chose to go to Milo, knowing what could happen, and that you would try to save me, and that you might not be able to get to me in time. I knew all those things, and I chose to go anyway."

She doesn't hate me for... *For*—such a small word, but important. She's not saying she doesn't hate me, just that she doesn't hate me for letting her make her own decisions.

She sighs as she leans back against the bathroom wall. And then she stares at the spot on the floor next to her, and I know what she wants. For me to sit next to her.

Does she understand how much it kills me right now to see her in so much pain and not be able to do anything about it?

Reluctantly, I move next to her and slide my back

against the wall until I'm sitting next to her, but not touching.

Kai stares off into the distance as she begins to speak. "My mind is fucked-up. Everything in my mind is twisted around. I can't tell what's real and what my mind has changed."

"What do you mean?"

She swallows. "When you rescued me—"

"I didn't rescue you. You were saving yourself long before I got there."

She scowls, shaking her head at me. So I shut up, but I don't want her to think I had anything to do with saving her. I didn't.

"When you came for me, my body was so damaged. But I swore I wouldn't let Milo win. I wouldn't let him take you from me. I wouldn't let myself stop loving you, no matter what I went through. I was desperate to fuck you. To wipe away any memories of Milo. But..." her voice shakes.

"But?" I need to hear this. I need to know how much of a mistake it was. Even though it was the closest I've ever felt to her. Because it felt like the first time we were making love instead of just fucking.

"But it twisted everything in my head, fucking you so close to what happened with Milo. My brain was still processing the rape. I was still processing the pain. And being with you just made it so much harder. It's why I have nightmares about you as much as I have nightmares about Milo. To my fucked up brain, the two events have melded into one event."

"I'm sorry. I should have known better."

She shakes her head. "I wouldn't change it. In that moment, I needed you."

"You just don't need me anymore."

She bites her lip.

"What else?" I ask, because I know there is more. If that was all that was hurting her, she would be trying to reprogram her brain. She wouldn't let Milo take me from her. There has to be more.

"Milo reminded of me of all the innocent people you have killed. You may save innocent women, but you've killed so many more than you ever saved."

I nod. "I'm the devil. I was raised by the devil, and then I became him. You are the only good thing in my life. I would say I regret killing the innocent people I've killed, but I don't. Because all I care about is you."

"I know, and I never meant to fall in love with the devil."

There is that word again—love.

"I know you haven't yet, but could you ever fall back in love with me?"

Her eyes meet mine. They are hard, dark, and unforgiving. She doesn't hate me because I couldn't stop Milo. She hates me because of who I am. I wish I could change, be the man she deserves, but I can't change enough for her. And I sure as hell can't change my past.

Kai doesn't answer me with words. And I know whatever love she felt is truly gone. *Fuck you, Milo.* If I could bring him back from the grave, I would. I need to kill him again myself.

Kai hates me, and she doesn't want to fight to change her feelings. There feels like there is more to the story, but she doesn't say.

I watch as Kai rubs her stomach.

"Are you going to be sick again?" I ask.

She shakes her head, and her hand immediately stops rubbing her stomach.

"What else? What else did Milo tell you?" I know there is more. I can see it. But I'm not sure she's ready to tell me.

"No, there's nothing else. Now you know the truth. I can never love you."

Lie.

Her words are all lies, but I don't call her out on it. If she's not ready to tell the truth, then that's fine. I don't get her truth. I haven't earned it yet. And I'm not sure I ever can.

I hear a light tap on the door edge—Langston.

He doesn't look at me. Instead, he looks at Kai as if asking if permission to enter.

She nods.

My time is up.

I stand up as Langston brings Kai the glass of water. I put my hand on his shoulder. "Thank you for taking care of her when I can't," I whisper so only he can hear me.

He nods solemnly.

And then I walk to the door, stopping and turning around one last time.

"Truth or lies, you hate me," I say.

"Truth," her voice breaks as she says it.

I turn and stare at her. But I can't tell if she is telling the truth or a lie.

"Truth or lies, I will never stop loving you," I say.

"I hope for your sake, that's a lie. Because there is nothing you could do to make me love you again," Kai says.

4

KAI

MY HEART ACHES WATCHING Enzo walk out the door. It shouldn't, but I hate him.

Or maybe I'm lying to myself?

I hate the nightmares. I hate how Enzo plays as much of a part in them as Milo does.

I hate how many people Enzo has killed. He killed his own half-brother, Pietro, even though he didn't know the relationship at the time. He still doesn't know of his relationship to Milo, or Pietro, or Felix. *Should I tell him?*

I hate how I can't protect him and the baby I carry at the same time. I protected Enzo in the past. And he protected me. But this baby is bigger than both of us.

And this baby in my stomach is at risk from everyone. No matter whose it is—Milo's or Enzo's.

It makes no difference. I will love the baby the same. I hate both men, so it doesn't really matter.

But this baby, I already love.

This baby gives me hope. Hope that the future doesn't have to be filled with violence, pain, and death.

If only I can hide this baby from the world.

Felix will try to get to this baby. To either kill it, if it's Enzo's to revenge his brother's death. Or to corrupt it, if the baby is Milo's, and use the baby to gain his own power in the Black empire.

Enzo will no doubt try to protect the baby and fail, because no matter how he tries to protect those he loves, he can't save them, not as long as he belongs to this dark world.

And the crew, the men and women who work for us, those I thought were on our side and loyal to a fault, will turn on us if this baby is Enzo's. There always has to be two heirs. One Miller and one Rinaldi. One from me and one from Enzo. This baby could be a mix of both. This baby would represent betrayal and disloyalty to them. They will kill the baby to ensure they destroy our love, as they have in previous generations. They won't understand Milo already did that. They won't understand Enzo is free to produce his own heir. That this baby is mine, and this child will take no part in this world—ever.

I refuse to let this baby be used as a pawn. I refuse to train this child to become the strongest to win a stupid battle for power.

Although, I know deep down I'm lying to myself. Because even if I lose the battle to become Black, I will still prepare my child for a possible future battle. I may not want them to become Mr. Black, but I will do everything I can to protect them. And that means preparing them for a battle, not to necessarily win, but to ensure they are strong enough to survive.

I rub my stomach absentmindedly as I climb back in bed with Langston lying next to me. And I know I won't be sleeping.

Enzo helped me sleep, but that's all I could tolerate. My body is at war with itself.

Hate and love playing equal parts.

I hate Enzo.

But despite Milo's best efforts, there is a part so deep inside that still clings to my love for Enzo.

I won't spark those feelings. I won't let them surface. My sole focus is on protecting my child, and Enzo only brings with him destruction, even if he doesn't intend to.

I need to live in the hate. I need to fight any coming feelings. I must protect my child from everyone. Even my own desperate love. I must. I'm a mother, and a mother will fight anyone who threatens her child.

———

I HAVEN'T LEFT my bedroom in days. I should get out. I need to figure out a plan. Because I need to get as far away from everyone as possible. I need to ensure Enzo becomes the next Mr. Black, as he was always destined to be. And then I need to disappear. Somewhere where no will ever find me.

Not Enzo.

Not Felix.

Not my father.

Not Langston.

Not even Liesel.

The only way to keep my child safe is to keep his or her identity under wraps. To hide the child from the world. Even from Enzo. He deserves to know the truth of the child, but he can never know.

I won't let my child go through any of the pain that Enzo and I had to go through to prepare for the games. My father fucking sold me to prepare me. And Enzo's father abused, beat, and trained him as a heartless soldier. No child of mine will ever go through that.

The Miller line will die with me. No one will know another Miller exists. I will be the end.

No one will battle for the Black empire anymore. Enzo and his children will gain full power—forever.

He'll probably have a child with Liesel, if the child Liesel spoke of isn't already Enzo's. It warms me to know he will end up with a woman who loves him and will take care of him when I'm gone.

I need to get off this yacht before I start showing. I'm only six or seven weeks. I have time. But the only way to escape without anyone following me is to finish the games. Only then can I ensure Enzo will be forced to let me go.

So I get dressed in shorts and a tank top, and for the first time in the last month, I leave the bedroom.

I walk up to the pool deck; the sun is blinding me as I step outside. But that's not what's burning my eyes. It's what I'm looking at, or really *whom*.

Liesel.

Langston.

Enzo.

All sitting on lounge chairs in swimsuits. All with a drink in their hand. All jaws dropping to the floor at the sight of me outside my bedroom.

I'm tired of letting Milo control me. I'm tired of letting my demons drive every decision I make. I'm tired, and I want this all to end.

"What are you—" Langston starts.

"Coming to get some sun? Good, your white ass needs some," Liesel says, cutting off Langston.

I nod. "Yes, I need to get some sun."

I take a seat next to Liesel. Enzo is the only one who is silent, but it doesn't matter. He's the only one I feel. But unlike hundreds of times before, it's not the electric connection pulling me to him that I feel. And I don't feel the heat emanating from his body.

He's cold, like me. I feel his pain. I feel his anger. I feel the heartbreak he's caused others. And I feel fear.

My breasts are crushed beneath his weight, until my chest is so heavy I can't get air.

My legs are spread wide, too wide.

And his length forces himself inside me, like a blade through my body. Slicing over and over.

I open my eyes, and I see the tears in Enzo's eyes as he watches me live a nightmare right in front of him.

I know it was Milo who hurt me, but when I close my eyes, it's Enzo. That has to be an omen. Milo and Enzo were half-brothers. The same darkness in Milo lives in Enzo. I can't trust him. I can't trust anyone.

"Sorry to interrupt the pool party, but I just wanted to let you know the fourth game will start tomorrow," Archard says out of nowhere.

Everyone's head snaps to him as he speaks, but as soon as he finishes, all eyes are on me.

I'm the wild card.

No one knows what I will do.

Will I fight to win?

Or will I purposely lose and let Enzo have the empire?

No one knows my truth.

Liesel and Langston may know my secret, but not how I

plan on playing the game.

They don't know how I will protect my secret—my child. Or my heart from falling for Enzo again. He's dangerous. Every time he's tried to save me, I've ended up getting hurt. He can't be trusted with a child, even if it's his.

5

———

ENZO

Watching Kai have nightmares about me, guts me. It's like living through a never-ending explosion, ripping my heart to tiny little pieces. Over and over. There is nothing left of my heart when I see her pain.

It's like Kai is strangling it, stabbing it, and drowning it all simultaneously, unable to decide which will inflict the worst pain on me.

I've felt so much pain in my life, but none worse than what I experience seeing Kai in pain. No training my father put me through could have prepared me for seeing her in this much pain.

Fuck.

This is the worst kind of punishment, and I deserve every drop of it. Kai may not be purposefully punishing me. She may not feel this is all my fault. But I know it is.

Kai's life before my world entered it wasn't perfect, far from it, but she saw a way out. She had a chance to get away, and instead of letting her go, I trapped her in this world.

I deserve so much worse than watching her in pain

because of me. I took the beautiful spark inside her and drowned it.

It's still there, I know it. She'll find it again, but without me. I've hurt her too many times. Failed her more than either of us can count. And loving her will only result in her early death. I've already risked her life too many times. Danger follows me wherever I go. And being one of the most powerful men in the world will draw my enemies to her. If my enemies know I love her, they will try to hurt her to get to me.

That's what this world does to people like us. We live a life of luxury, but one where we are always looking over our shoulder to see who wants to kill us. We always have to be at the top of our game to survive.

This shouldn't be Kai's life. I love her, and loving her means I have to be strong enough to protect her, which means getting her as far away from me as possible. Because I will suck the life out of her.

Tomorrow the fourth game starts. I'm currently winning two to one. Tomorrow I could clinch the win. Then all that would be left is sorting out heirs and completing the paperwork for the next generation of competitors.

Please let the game tomorrow be kind to Kai.

I don't care if she wins or loses. I'll support whatever she wants. But I can't let this game hurt her. She's already hurting too much.

Please let it not risk her life, not hurt her.

Who am I kidding? My father created this game. It will be the worst kind of pain. The worst kind of torture.

The sun seems to stretch out infinitely, the day moving slower than any days before. Kai stays outside soaking in every ray of sun with us. None of us speak to each other. We just drink, like alcohol is the only thing to take away all of our pain.

We all have torment for different reasons. But the only pain I'm focused on is Kai's. She is my everything. My sun and my night. My reason for living and my reason for dying.

I've failed before. I won't fail again. She will never suffer again. I will not let it happen.

From now on, she is my queen. She is no longer a stingray. She will no longer have to use her stinger to protect herself. I will lay down everything for her.

The men and women who work for the organization may think I'm the best leader for them. They are wrong. I'm the worst. Because I will put Kai above all their lives. Maybe at one time I would have made a great leader, but not anymore.

These games are a waste.

Kai doesn't want to become Black.

And I only want to use the power to protect her.

Neither of us is worthy of the title.

Neither of us will do the job required of us.

Neither of us will be selfless enough to run a powerful empire, using the power to protect the lives that work for us.

Finally, the sun begins to set, and Kai gets up from her chair. I watch her disappear inside silently. Liesel follows next. Then eventually Langston.

I'm alone.

I'm always alone.

I've lived alone, and I'll die alone.

That is my fate.

I get up off my chair, every bone in my body throbbing. It only seems fair my heart is broken like every other part of my body. So many bones have been broken I'm not even sure how my body is staying together. My skin has been stitched, my bones put in casts, blood pumped into my body. But none of those things truly healed me. I'll always be broken. And that's how my heart feels, unable to be repaired.

I walk through the hallways of the yacht until I reach Kai's door. I lean against the door, considering knocking. I just need to see her face. I need to breathe the same air as her. Because my time with her is running out. This could be the end of her existence in my life.

But I've been too selfish when it comes to her. So I don't knock.

Instead, I slide down the floor and sit outside her door.

I pull my phone out of my pocket and pull up the security camera in her room. I've never used it before. But I need to see her now.

Kai is lying in the bed. Her eyes are closed, and her breathing is steady, but I don't think she's sleeping.

Langston is lying shirtless next to her, studying her to see if she's asleep. After twenty minutes of watching her steady breathing, he decides she's asleep. He rolls over and is out within minutes.

As soon as Langston starts snoring, Kai's eyes pop open. She wasn't asleep. She just didn't want Langston worrying about her.

Oh, stingray.

She takes the scrunchie out of her hair and starts fidgeting with it.

She should have fallen for a man like Zeke. He was still involved in this world, but the second she became his, he would have given it all up for her. He could have gotten a normal job as an accountant, or engineer, or salesman. Anything to provide stability to her. He would have married her, had kids with her, protected her. Bought her a gorgeous house in the suburbs. Learned to make friends with the neighbors and take the kids to soccer practice. Even coached the little league team.

He would have been the husband and father I could never be.

Kai should have been with a man like Zeke. Instead, I took away any chance she had. But I will give it back to her. I promise.

Kai continues to fidget with the scrunchie, no doubt missing Zeke. I should have died that day instead of him. He would have gotten her away from Milo. She would have been safe.

And then I see it. The tiny heart I carved for her. It's still on the scrunchie, not only that, but it's what she is fidgeting and focusing on. The heart, not the scrunchie. She's thinking of me.

Her eyes flitter up to the corner of the room, as if she knows there is a camera there, even though she can't see it. Her eyes glaze to mine as I watch her.

My connection to her is still there even if hers is gone, but for a moment I think she feels it too. Our old connection that breaks through walls, time, and space to reach each other.

But she quickly breaks the connection. She slips the scrunchie back on her wrist and then closes her eyes, as sleep quickly takes her.

Sleep, my queen. You don't have to worry anymore. I will protect you, even at my own expense.

I watch her breath change from easy to fast, and I immediately know what's happening.

My hand reaches for the doorknob, but I stop.

If I go to her, I'll make her nightmare worse.

Wake up, Langston.

Protect her.

There is nothing I can do but wait.

My hand rests on the wooden door, trying to feel all her pain. Hoping if I feel it, she won't have to.

She tosses in bed, wrestling with an imaginary man.

It doesn't take Langston long to stir. He grabs her and pulls her to his body, trying to warm her and bring her out of the nightmare.

But she doesn't immediately stop her thrashing.

I grip the door harder, willing the universe to give me all of her pain.

I stare at the tiny image of her on my phone as her nightmare gets worse.

No. Please, no. Make it stop.

Tears. Tears cascade down my cheeks, flooding my face. Running over my lips and off my chin.

I've never been a man who cries, but for her, I cry. I don't care if the emotions make me weak. Before her, I thought the tears and emotions made me a pussy. Made me weak. But I realize now my love for her makes me stronger than I've ever been before. Maybe if I'd given in to the feelings after our first encounter in that bar, I would have saved her from all of this.

But I didn't. And I don't get a do-over. I don't get to turn back time and save her.

She went through hell.

Now it's my turn.

I sit silently outside her door—my hell. The fire consumes me as I watch her slowly come out of her nightmare. Langston protects her with his body. I've never been jealous of Langston before, but I am now. I wish I were him. I wish I could feel her in my arms again. Just one more time.

Instead, I suffer alone.

Tomorrow this could end. I could win the final game. I could become Mr. Black. I could take over the empire as I was always destined to. And then I would have the power to protect her.

I would send Langston and a dozen of my best men to protect her. And then I would send her far away from here. I would hide her, even from myself because as long as I knew where she was, I would come for her. My love is too great to stay away. And I'm her greatest enemy. I have to give her up. But when the time comes, will I have the strength to do it?

6

———

KAI

I GO THROUGH THE MOTIONS.

I shower.

I get dressed.

I eat breakfast.

But my heart isn't really in it. I don't want to win the game; I just want this to be over.

All of it.

I stand in front of the mirror, gripping my flat stomach that will soon hold a bump. *How long can I keep this a secret? How much time will it take for my little baby to be visible?*

I try not to ignore the game, but that's all I could think about last night.

The last game gave me a broken leg, a dislocated shoulder, and more stab wounds. Enzo faired worse—almost dying.

Either one of us could have died during that game. It was by far the most dangerous either of us has faced so far. My father created that game.

What will be coming now that Enzo's father created this next chapter?

Whatever the game is, it will be far more dangerous than any of the previous. And unlike every other time, my only focus is on surviving.

I walk out of the bedroom and find everyone on the main deck of the yacht. I notice land in the distance. Not just any land, my home—Miami.

Miami may have been my home, but it's not a place I plan on staying in when this is all over. Miami has not treated any of us well.

An ominous feeling settles on the group as I walk closer. All of us are exhausted; we just what this over. We are tired and weary and don't want to fight anymore.

Maybe it can be over?

Archard is standing at the end of the yacht with papers to read us in his hand.

"What happens if I withdraw?" I ask.

Liesel smiles.

Langston's mouth falls wide.

And Enzo frowns.

I don't know why any of them care if I withdraw. They all know Enzo is the better person to run the organization. I want nothing to do with it. I want to get as far away from here as possible.

"At this point in the game, I would highly recommend you don't withdraw," Archard says in a mysterious tone. He doesn't tell me why I shouldn't withdraw. He doesn't say I can't withdraw. Just that he recommends I don't.

All eyes are on me, as more dark clouds roll overhead. Something dark is coming. My whole life is nothing but darkness, so it doesn't shock me. But Milo is dead. My biggest threat is gone. All that is left is finishing this stupid game.

Something deep in my gut tells me not to withdraw. So I don't say anything further.

Archard hitches an eyebrow looking directly at me. "Should I start?"

I nod.

And then Liesel and Langston's eyes are on Archard, not on me. But Enzo stays focused on me, like I'm his whole world. Hiding my pregnancy from him is going to be near impossible. He knows everything about me. And even if our connection isn't what it used to be, he still can see through any lie I tell.

I need to get out of here before he finds out.

"This round was created by Enzo's father to test your bravery, courage, and self-sacrifice," Archard says.

Enzo snorts. "My father knew nothing about any of those qualities."

Archard ignores him, choosing to continue speaking. "This game will test all of those qualities and more. The winner of this round won't be decided by me. The winner will be chosen by a team of five people selected to represent the men and women who work for you."

What?

Every game before has been very straightforward. Very easy to determine the winner. But this time we will be judged by a team of people who work for us. This doesn't even seem fair, if I cared about winning. Enzo has grown up in this world, around these people. He knows them on a personal level. Of course, they would vote for him over me.

"I will introduce you to the five people deciding your fate after I finish discussing the rules. The game will last one month. This is a test to see who is the better leader. Each of you will take turns leading the Black empire, and proving you are the best fit for the job."

This seems too easy. *We just do the job we've already been doing but individually?*

"Enzo will be the first to have his leadership abilities tested. Each night the five-member team will vote to decide if he has done a good enough job to stay in power or if Kai should take over," Archard continues.

"Wait, Kai doesn't even get a chance to prove herself unless Enzo screws up? That doesn't seem fair," Liesel says.

"This game isn't fair. It was created by Enzo's father, so of course it will favor him," Archard says, defiance in his eyes.

Liesel growls back and looks like she's about to punch Archard, but Langston steps in, wrapping his arms around Liesel which only ignites her further.

"It's fine, I don't need a fair fight in order to win," I say. But I don't want to win. I just want out of here.

Liesel relaxes before pushing Langston away from her.

"What's the catch?" Enzo asks.

"What do you mean?" Archard asks.

"I mean, this is too easy. Just do the job we are both competing to do. That's it? That's too easy and doesn't involve much danger. So what's the catch?" Enzo asks again.

Archard sighs reading over the papers again. "A month isn't a long time. You could have a relatively easy month, which wouldn't test your abilities fairly. So your father arranged a series of events guaranteed to happen during the month-long period. But the events will be very real, with real-life consequences."

"Of course, he did," Enzo sighs, shaking his head as if his father could see his disappointment.

This game could be more dangerous than all the rest. Because the game is all about surprise. Who knows what event we will face. What enemies he's sparked to attack. For the next month, we will never be safe. And I don't know if it's better I sit on the sidelines, or try to lead myself to ensure my own safety.

"One last thing before I introduce you to the judges. Remember, it doesn't matter who wins this game, whether it's Enzo or Kai. After the game is over, you will both have a year to produce an heir. And then the final task has to be completed. If Enzo wins this game, he would simply have to complete the final task solo in order to win. If Kai wins, the games are tied, which means you will both compete in the final round. Either way, a blood heir has to be found."

Archard doesn't say what will happen if neither of us produce an heir, but I'm guessing from how the games have worked so far, it wouldn't be good.

"Any questions?" Archard asks.

I have a million—*like why the hell this stupid game was invented in the first place? What happened to cause this entire sequence of events?* But I don't ask.

"Good, Enzo will take charge first. And as I said, if the five crew members decide you are doing a bad job or that they want to give Kai a chance to lead for any reason, they will take a vote at the end of the day. Any other questions?" Archard repeats himself.

His eyes flitter around the room. "Good." He whistles and four men and one woman start climbing the ladder up the side of the yacht.

Enzo frowns. He doesn't like anyone getting on his yacht without his permission.

"I'm Clifton, head of intelligence," he first man says. His skin is light, his hair shaved, and his clothes are glued to his thick muscles.

"I'm Denziel, head of technology," the next man says.

He's much smaller than the first, with pale skin, and very little muscle.

"I'm Vance, head sailor," the next man barks. His voice is rough, just like his exterior. His clothes already look dirty, and his skin is much darker, like he spends all his time in the sun.

"I'm Ulysses, debt collector." This man is by far the biggest. In some ways he reminds me of Zeke. He's all big and brawn. But for some reason, I'm not sure he will be as much of the teddy bear Zeke was. His eyes look crueler.

The woman steps forward. She's in the same uniform of dark pants, boots, and a gray T-shirt. "I'm Odette, in charge of security." She may be a woman, but she seems just as fierce as all the others on the team.

Enzo nods at all of them. And they all nod back at him, placing their arms behind their backs as they await his orders. They all show him respect, and I have no doubt they all respect him as a leader. It's a good thing I don't want the job, because I would be screwed.

In a way, it makes me wonder why we are playing the games if everyone in the organization wants Enzo to be their leader. *Did I ever really have a chance? If I had won, would they all revolt against me anyway?*

It doesn't matter now.

I should just go slink back into my room and hide away for the next month. Let Enzo do his thing. Prove even further that he deserves to Mr. Black. He's always been Enzo Black, since birth. He never went by his true last name of Rinaldi. He was born into this, while I was born into nothing.

I am nothing.

I am no one.

Which will make it easier to disappear.

I take a step back as Enzo makes small talk with the men and woman who boarded his yacht. He's already drilling them on the status of everything, and I hear him correct one of them when they answer incorrectly. How has he had time to keep up with all the day to day operations with everything else going on?

I don't know, and I don't care. I just want to go hide away in my room where it's safe.

I take another step back and another. If I didn't hate Enzo so much, I would almost admire how the team falls in line with him at the helm. But I don't admire him; my heart hates him. So I don't notice that.

Another step back.

And then I turn.

And run into a hard chest.

I bounce off it, and I see his hands rise to stabilize me, but they stop midair. He won't touch me without my permission.

"How did you—?" I start, not able to understand how Enzo moved from one side of the deck to the other in a matter of seconds without me hearing him.

He shrugs. "I've been trained many years to be able to do that. I can move silently so no one, enemies nor allies, can hear me. I wasn't able to sneak up on you before. Our connection was too great. You could tell anytime I moved, but now..." his voice is sad as he trails off.

I nod. "I was just heading back to my room. It seems I'm not really needed for this game. You've already won."

"Just because the crew knows me better, doesn't give me an automatic win. If you want me to win, I will. If you want me to ensure you get a fighting chance during this game, I will. If you want me to go full force into competition mode and do everything I can to defeat you while you compete back, I will. Just tell me what to do, stingray."

Enzo puts his hands in his pockets and looks down at me with so much hope in his eyes. I don't know what he's hoping for, just that his eyes are big, his expression is soft, and there's a hint of a dimple in the corner of his cheek. He wants to smile at me so badly, but won't let himself.

All I see when I look at him now is a monster. A monster who has killed. A monster who was just as capable of hurting me like Milo did. A man who did hurt me, almost as badly as Milo.

"You can't hide away yet, Kai. Soon, baby, you can hide away in the most remote place on earth. After this is over, I'll make sure it happens if that is what you want. But I don't want you to live with regrets. The life of hiding may be what you want, and I don't blame you if it is. But despite what you may think, you were built for this life. I think you are just as capable, if not more so, of living in this world and shining. You are strong and just and loyal and brave. All the traits a good leader needs. The Black empire has done some bad things, but you might be the only person who could turn it into something good."

I can't stay. Maybe if it was just me, I would try. I would fight to get my feelings for Enzo back. I would fight to see if I was a capable leader. But this baby means I don't get to be cavalier with my life. I have to protect this new life at all costs.

"Let me show you how beautiful this world can be. Let me introduce you to the people that work for us. Show you how human and powerful this job can be, then you can decide," he says.

But I can read between the lines. He wants me with him so he can protect me. He doesn't know what we are about to face for the next month. And if I'm here unprotected, I'm at risk.

I'll do anything to protect my baby.

I look into the depths of Enzo's eyes, reaching down to his soul. And for some reason in this moment, I truly believe Enzo is the only person who is capable of protecting me.

"Okay."

7

ENZO

It FEELS like everything in my life has been moving toward this moment. This game will most likely be our last together. If I win, I just have to complete the final task, produce an heir, and I return to living my life as Enzo Black.

Powerful.

Wealthy.

Lonely.

Those are the three words that described my life before Kai. And they will describe my life after her. I'm living on limited time. I know she's going to go. But I'm afraid her disappearing won't be as freeing as she wants it to be.

She will always be looking over her shoulder. Every damn day one of my enemies will find her.

She will never feel safe.

Maybe she won't feel safe if she became Kai Black, one of the most powerful people of the underground. But at least she would have the power to control her own destiny.

Whatever she chooses, I want it to be her own choice.

And until she's officially made the choice, I want her with me.

To keep her safe.

And because as much as I try to be selfless when I'm around her, I'm selfish. I want her with me. Even if I don't get to touch her. Even if all I get to do is crave her. If all I get is to breathe the same air. I want her near me. And I want to heal her before she leaves.

Kai may think she's broken, but she's thought that before. I don't care who heals her—Liesel, Langston, or me. I don't care if she finds a way to realize how whole she is all by herself. But I can't let her go until the nightmares have diminished. Until she can walk in both the light and dark again. Until she's the queen she was always meant to be.

And her one little word, returned my hope—okay.

Not hope that she could love me again, just hope that she's going to be just that—okay.

Only then will I be able to let her go. I thought I freed her before. It was a lie. This time, when I let her go, it will be real, permanent. My life will be empty from that moment on.

Kai follows me back to the group still gathered on my yacht. I don't like any of them here without my permission. And I tell them that with the way I stomp back.

I haven't been in control of day to day operations in a while. Langston has done a lot for me, and I've given each individual head control of their section. It hasn't been important to demand perfection from all of them when I was dealing with so many personal things. And I would have had to involve Kai in every single decision.

Now, I don't have to.

A tiny thrill at having my full power back jolts down my spine. I like the power. I like being in charge. I like being commanding.

And I've missed it.

I glance behind me at the woman standing behind me who looks more timid than I've seen her in a long time.

And I would trade it all way to have one more hour with her.

I square my shoulders back to the small crowd. I can't let them see the love I have for her. My vulnerability. If I do, then they might mistake it for weakness.

I don't know whether Kai is going to try to compete in this game or not. But I have this uncontrollable desire to try and win. I like winning; I like power; it's bred into my pores.

"What are you all still doing here? Don't you have a job to do?" I growl, my voice practically shaking the yacht.

All five of my crew members stand taller. "Yes, sir," they say in unison, as they start to head toward the edge of the yacht.

"Wait," Archard says.

They all freeze, but are clearly terrified. I punish my team for disobedience or disloyalty. I'm the only person whose orders they follow. I've killed men who didn't follow my orders when it risked others' lives.

Quickly, they realize their mistake when they see my snarl and start moving again, ignoring Archard.

"Fucking wait, you cowards," Archard screams.

They all look at him but keep moving. They won't stop until I give them the word to.

Archard huffs in frustration. "Will you tell them to stop? They can't judge you if you order them away."

I give one nod, and all five of them stop.

Archard exhales, clearly frustrated by the whole scene. He thinks he has power because he's the company lawyer and is ensuring the contract is enacted. That doesn't mean he holds any power. As soon as the games are over, I'm firing his ass.

"They must remain near enough to judge your actions every day," Archard says.

"How are they supposed to do their jobs if they are following me around all the time?" I bark.

"It's the rules. I didn't create them. They don't have to follow every move you make, but if you stay on this yacht, they need to be on the yacht. If you go to one of the bars you own, they can follow in their own cars. And they will have to lead their individual teams from wherever you are or assign a new person to lead in their absence."

All five pairs of eyes glare at Archard. They all worked hard for their jobs. They won't give up their positions easily, not even for a month.

My eyes cut to them. "Lead from afar."

Five pairs of shoulders relax, and they no longer act like they want to kill Archard. "But if a crisis happens, if we are attacked, if something happens under your jurisdiction, then you drop this stupid game responsibilities and do your damn job or you're fired. You may be able to judge me, but I have the power to decide whether you still have a job or not. I still have the power to decide if you are punished or not. Understand?"

"Yes, Mr. Black." Their voices ring together.

Black. They already think of me as Black—their leader.

Maybe threatening them doesn't sound like the best way to get them to vote for me to be their leader. But they all respect me for it. They know I would jump in front of a bullet for them.

A phone buzzes in Clifton's pocket. He looks horrified, but reluctantly pulls it out of his pocket to answer.

He turns his back and mumbles into the phone so none of us can hear his conversation.

I take a moment to glance at Kai. She's standing reluctantly on the deck, looking at Clifton curiously like he might tell her Milo has come back from the dead and we are going to have to fight him. She's always going to be looking over her shoulder, waiting for ghosts to attack her —her father, Milo, Justin, my father, even me. No man has ever treated her well.

That's not true—Zeke was the only man who was truly kind to her and treated her like the queen she is. But he left us all too soon. He's a guy like all the rest of us. He would have eventually failed her, just as all of us did.

At least she has one good man to hold onto. One good memory.

Clifton hangs up and stares at me. His nostrils are wide as he pants heavily, his face is white, and his eyes bulge.

"What is it, Clifton?" I ask, I try to keep my voice calm, but I'm in no mood to be patient. If he has something to tell me, he needs to say it.

"That was um...that was..."

"Spit it out," I stomp over to him, getting in his face. I'm sure it won't help him answer quicker, but I don't care. I'm frustrated with my life. Every time I try to do right by Kai, I end up fucking everything up. And I would never take that anger out on her, but I can on Clifton.

"That was Phin, the captain of *The Reverent,* sir. He's headed this way."

"Why?"

He swallows down the lump in his throat. *Please don't let that be vomit.* If he vomits on me, he's a dead man.

"He said he wants to challenge you. That you haven't been doing a good job of leading us lately. That he could do a better job."

"He wants to challenge me," I say slowly, a light air to my voice.

He nods. "To become the leader of the Black empire."

I laugh. It's a full belly laugh. I'm hysterical, because this is the most ridiculous thing I've ever heard. I've been fighting to be Mr. Black my entire life, and Phin thinks with one fight he could take that all away from me. He's insane.

"He can't do that though. That's not how it works," Kai says.

I stop laughing long enough to look at her. Her face is pale, but her voice is strong.

I raise an eyebrow as I turn back to Clifton. "Did you tell him that's not how this works?"

"Yes, but he wouldn't listen. He said he had to come here and fight you. It was time."

I smirk. Of course, today is the day. *Father*. He orchestrated this. *How many people did he plant or bribe into attacking me over the next month? How many people will I have to fight to protect what belongs to Kai and me?*

"You can't fight him," Kai says, her tone would be unreadable to everyone else. The pulse in her neck beats faster. And her breath hitches at a more rapid pace. And her eyes pierce my heart as if the piece of my heart I gave her is guiding her actions now.

Maybe she has more feelings toward me than she realizes.

"Don't worry, baby. No one can hurt me without my permission. You are the only one allowed to hurt me. You are the only one who can."

8

———

KAI

My heart clenches at the thought of Enzo fighting.

Why do I care?

He has nothing to do with me. I don't love him. He's hurt me so many times, and my baby relies on him not knowing about the pregnancy. I probably shouldn't have even told Liesel, but I needed to tell someone. And now I have to live with the consequences.

I can't love Enzo.

Loving him would make it easier for him to find out about the baby. And whether Enzo wanted my child brought into this dangerous world or not, he wouldn't have a choice. He couldn't protect the child from this life. These men and women would come for my child. They always have to have a leader. The strongest. My heir and Enzo's facing off and continuing through generations.

I can't love Enzo, even if I wanted to. I have no doubt these five people standing on the deck would put a stop to it. Milo told the story. The look in these five pairs of eyes confirms it. Archard has said as much when discussing the contract.

I can't love Enzo.

So why is my heart fluttering at the thought of Enzo getting hurt? I thought Milo fixed my problem for feeling anything for this man.

It's just because I'm a good person, and I don't want any man to feel any pain. But looking around at the deck, I know I wouldn't care if any of the rest of the men got punched in the face. I wouldn't mind watching any of them bleed.

I spot the other yacht pulling up in the distance. I cover my eyes from the sun as I stare at the shiny black yacht that stops next to us.

Liesel stands next to me, as Langston approaches Enzo and whispers something to him.

"What are they talking about?" I ask, Liesel.

"Langston is concerned the attacks are going to get worse each day until the month is over. He wants to gather any members of the crew and allies we trust and put them on high alert to be ready to fight with Enzo. We think Enzo's father put several sleeper agents on the team for this very challenge. There are only a limited number of people we can trust," Liesel says.

I nod. I was thinking the same thing.

"Good, I don't want Enzo to get hurt."

Liesel gives me a side-eyed glance. "You holding up?"

I nod.

"Good, you can't let Enzo know. You can't trust him. He's failed you before. All you can trust is yourself."

Her words ring true. I can only trust myself. I can't trust her. And I know despite her understanding my situation that she has ulterior motives. She loves the same man I used to love—Enzo. And with me out of the picture, she can move in and earn his love. She might carry his child one day after all. While I most likely carry the child of his devil of a half-brother.

I put my hand on my stomach. *It doesn't matter who you came from, little one, you belong to me and I'll love you all the same.*

Which is why I can't fight for this empire either. My baby comes first. And I won't risk my child's life to save an empire.

This is Enzo's fight. And hopefully, I'm never given a chance to fight in this challenge. They all love Enzo. He just needs to prove how strong and powerful he is, because I don't trust what challenges and obstacles Enzo's father might have put in our way.

I hear the roar of the small engine of the dingy boat as it makes its way from one yacht to the other. It purrs to a stop, as waves crash in its wake.

Enzo and Langston continue to chat and form a plan as footsteps ascend the ladder.

The five crew members in charge of judging, all take giant steps back.

That can't be good.

They seem afraid of whoever is climbing the ladder. I know they are afraid of Enzo, too, but with the right amount of balance between fear, respect, and loyalty. They trust Enzo to make the right decision with their lives.

Whoever is climbing up the stairs, they just fear.

Liesel and I both suck in a breath when the man hits the top rung of the ladder.

Holy fuck.

I bite my lip to keep from screaming at the man on the deck. He can't be the man who wants to challenge Enzo. Maybe he's the man's bodyguard or something.

This man is tall, like giant tall. Easily six foot six or

taller. His head is shaved, and tattoos cover his entire muscular body. I don't see a drop of fat anywhere. His hands are covered in grime, and it's clear he uses them to get shit done. He's not one of the men who manages a team from an office somewhere. He leads with the power of his body, not his mind.

Enzo is tall. Enzo has muscles, I remind myself.

But this man has a couple of inches in height—several pounds of additional muscle. And more grit than Enzo ever thought of having.

Enzo finishes his conversation with Langston—who nods and then pulls out his cell phone to start making calls as he disappears inside the yacht. He doesn't seem worried at all by the new man's appearance. So I shouldn't either.

Except I'm terrified for Enzo.

Enzo is all business as he calmly walks over to greet the man who dared to step foot on his yacht unannounced. To my surprise, Enzo extends his hand to the man, but the way the new man grips it, most likely draining his hand of blood, I know it's not a friendly shake.

"Phin," Enzo says.

The man just nods back.

"What are you doing? You don't need to do this. You are just wasting both of our times. You can't challenge me for leadership. That's not how this works. Even if you win, it will change nothing."

"It's not about winning. It's ensuring you are still strong enough to lead."

"How much did my father pay you to do this?" Enzo says, letting him know he knows the truth.

"Plenty, but I would do this for free," he says.

"You know the consequences if you lose. This action can't go unpunished."

"I don't plan on losing."

"Then that's foolish; you should always plan on losing. Not everyone can win all the time. Everyone loses. You might win, but this could be the time you lose. Do you really want to pay with your life?"

The man ignores Enzo and steps forward. "I want to challenge Enzo for leadership. I understand if I win, I won't become Mr. Black, but then I never was a mister anything. But I want to prove to you all, that Enzo isn't fit for the title either."

"You do understand if Enzo is deemed unfit to be leader, the job would fall to Kai?" one of the crewmen says.

I glare at him. I need to protect myself and stay out of this game, but I don't like being treated like a weakling by any misogynist.

I open my mouth, but Enzo steps in. "Don't talk about Kai that way. She's more than capable of being a leader. She would do a better job than I would. So don't act like she's less than."

"She?" Phin says. His eyes travel to mine.

I glare at him as I stand taller. I will not let him think less of me. I'm strong. I'm powerful. I could lead this organization easily. I am worthy.

He smirks at me.

"If she'd rather challenge me, I'd gladly swap her for you, Enzo."

I frown.

Even if I had a gun and this man had no weapon, I'd lose. He'd beat the crap out of me, and I'd lose my child. I can't fight him, even if I want to put him in his place.

"Beating up on a woman doesn't make you worthy," Enzo says to Phin.

He smirks.

"What are the rules of your challenge?" Enzo asks.

"Rules? There are no rules. We fight to the death," Phin says.

"The death, really? You're willing to risk your life against me, all to prove I'm not worthy?"

"Yes," the man grins, revealing teeth that look like they've been shaved into points. The tattoos around his eyes turn into sharp horns ready to ram into Enzo.

No rules.

Death.

That means they can use any weapon. They can use any other person to help them. They can cheat, play dirty. Everything goes. Which means this won't be fair. Enzo was blind-sided with this challenge. Phin was prepared. He will be ruthless in his pursuit.

Please, Enzo back out. Don't accept his challenge. Shoot him dead before the challenge even starts. Do something, just don't die.

"You're a fool, Phin," Enzo sighs.

Yes, he's not going to accept. The crew will understand. They won't vote him out and me in. It would take a lot for them to vote me, a girl, as their leader. Enzo would have to fuck up, lose hundreds of men to an enemy kind of fuck up. Not accepting a stupid challenge won't make them vote me in.

Enzo holds out his hand again. "I accept."

Phin smirks, shaking his hands.

I gasp.

Liesel shouts, "No, this is stupid! Don't fight!"

But her cries go unnoticed. The men are already locked in a battle where only one will survive. Enzo's father hired a crew member to fight Enzo to the death. *How fucked up is that?*

Draw your gun, Enzo! What are you waiting for?

Apparently, weapons are reserved for later in the fight. Testosterone has taken over, and both men drive hard at full force toward the other with nothing but their bodies to attack their opponent with.

"I can't watch," I whisper, my hands flying up to my face.

I hear the impact like a crack of thunder in the distance.

I spread my fingers, allowing my eyes to see through the slits.

Blood spurts everywhere from the two men. I'm shocked to see them both still upright after the collision. I expected Enzo to be knocked on his ass. His frame is too small to win a hand to hand combat fight against this giant.

Enzo spits blood—probably from a loose tooth.

Slowly, I lower my hands. I can't watch. But I have to watch.

Phin slowly pulls back his fist and tries to throw everything he has into punching Enzo in the jaw.

Enzo ducks easily, the punch moving far too slow to make contact.

My shoulders relax just a little. Phin may be stronger, but Enzo is faster, and hopefully smarter. To win, Enzo just has to tire the giant out. Enzo has had a lot of practice against Zeke, who was a giant in his own right. *He can do this. He has to.*

More swings, more ducks.

"Are you just going to dance around or are you going to fight me?" Phin says.

"It's not my fault you can't land a punch," Enzo says cockily back, not even bothering to try to get his own punches in.

Phin gets annoyed with Enzo's antics. I don't know what he's going to do, but I can tell things are about to escalate.

As quick as I've seen the giant move, he pulls something from his pocket and slings it at Enzo.

"No!" I shout.

Enzo tries to move out of the way of the blade, but it still hits his arm.

I can't breathe.

There is a knife in Enzo's arm. It doesn't look too deep. But I can't stand this fight.

Enzo grins as he pulls the knife out. "Thanks for the weapon." He grips the knife, and this time, he goes on the offensive. He hits Phin in the hands several times as the man tries to block Enzo's cuts.

I wince at all the blood oozing off of Phin's hands.

Enzo has this.

But then just as I think Enzo will win easily, Phin grabs his wrist and forces the knife from Enzo's hand. And then he punches Enzo over and over as he grips his wrist. Enzo tries to duck, but Phin anticipates this and punches lower. Hitting him in the face and stomach.

I gasp as Enzo's eye turns purple, and his mouth swells with blood.

The crew can barely watch.

Liesel stands frozen, unable to watch yet unable to stop watching. She's speechless, unusual for her. She's as terrified as I am.

Phin changes his tactic from punching to kicking with his steel-toed boot—doing serious damage to Enzo's stomach.

Dammit, stop him Enzo.

I know he can take pain. I've seen him in worse situations before, but it still makes me sick.

I grip my stomach as the queasiness washes from my stomach up my throat.

I will not be sick. I will not be sick.

But I know it's only a matter of time. The morning sickness combined with the anxiety of watching Enzo getting beat up and knowing there is nothing I can do is too much.

Enzo spots me from the corner of his eye. His face pales for a second when he sees me in this much pain, and then he winks at me.

He fucking winks. *How is that supposed to make any of this better?*

Stop fucking around and kick this guy's ass, I mouth sternly.

He laughs.

I shake my head sternly. No laughing. Stop making me care about you. I can't care about you. *What don't you get?*

Enzo smiles and then in one quick movement he gets out of Phin's hold and quickly fires several punches back until Phin looks like the bloodied one and Enzo looks like the stronger.

I smile, *thank you.*

Enzo sweeps the knife off the floor and then kicks Phin to the floor, pressing the knife against Phin's neck.

"This is your last chance, surrender and I'll let you live, although you will be punished for your actions," Enzo says, barely breaking a sweat, while Phin pants heavily, drenched in blood, sweat, and his own loss.

"Never," he says, his eyes flickering somewhere. And that's when all hell breaks loose.

Men attack the boat from every angle. Guns drawn, knives in their hands, or just their fists curled.

At least a dozen. This has gone from an unfair fight to a complete ambush. Unfair isn't a strong enough word for what is happening.

Enzo simply laughs as he draws his own gun.

"Really? You can't even fight me one on one; you need a dozen men to back you up?" Enzo laughs more.

Stop laughing and start killing men.

Enzo looks around at the room at men, who I assume work for him. "Surrender now, and you get to live. I understand you all loved and respected my father as leader, and you want to do your part to ensure I'm just as strong, but this isn't necessary. We have enough enemies I can prove my strength against."

Enzo waits, but he already knows none of the men will back down.

Langston moves to back up Enzo, but Enzo shakes his head.

My heart stops. He wants to do this himself. *Why won't he let Langston help him?*

"Fine," Enzo says, not waiting for them to attack. He fires his gun rapidly, and men start dropping.

Bullets fly all around me, and Liesel jerks my arm as we dive under a table. Langston runs to our side, using his body to shield us. He pulls his gun but doesn't fire it. Just using it to protect us.

"Fire your gun," I yell at Langston.

"Enzo would kick my ass for interfering in his fight. He has this. He's fought more men than this by himself before. His father trained him well," Langston says.

"Still, he doesn't need to risk his life like this. He doesn't need to be such a show-off," I say.

Langston stills, staring down at me. "You change your mind about your feelings?"

"No."

"Good."

I hide behind Langston's shoulder, not afraid of the bullets for myself but for my child. But needing to know

Enzo is still standing. A few stray shards hit him, but he doesn't seem fazed. The men that survived the initial string of bullets move closer and begin hand to hand combat.

One grabs Enzo's neck from behind as two others punch from the front, and yet two more try to grab Enzo's arms.

I'm going to be sick.

My stomach burns with acid and anxiety. This can't be happening. Enzo can't fight off this many men.

"Trust him. He does this for a living. I've seen him do this countless times. He's the best fighter I've ever seen. Brave to a fault. He never lets anyone else risk their life for him. He won't let me or anyone else he cares about. And he won't die."

I watch in horror as three men hold him while two start their ring of punches.

"He can't get out of that," I whisper, doubting him.

Langston shakes his head. "Just watch."

Sure enough, Langston is right. Enzo swings his legs up, kicking both men punching him back hard to the ground, he head butts the guy clinging to his neck and then twists his arms free of the other two before clunking their heads together.

He fires his gun twice before punching several more. His moves are fluid like an orchestrated dance he's done thousands of times.

I feel him again for the first time since I got on this yacht. His heart rate is slow and steady. Blood pumps warm through his body but not so hot that it makes him unable to move. The adrenaline is just enough to keep him fighting.

I no longer doubt he can win, but I still don't like it. Enzo shouldn't have to risk his life.

He takes down all five men that attacked him at once, and it seems like the fight is almost over.

Liesel says something, but I don't hear it.

Langston turns to say something to her, his grip on his gun loosened.

Phin is all that is left. Enzo pants heavily holding his own gun limp in his hand, his back to Phin. I know he's waiting for him to fire and then Enzo will fire back.

But I'm pissed.

This shouldn't have happened in the first place. Every drop of blood Enzo spilled is because of Phin. And I won't let anyone else hurt my man. Not one drop of blood.

Never again.

I may not be able to love Enzo. I may not be able to put him first in my life. But right now I can do something to protect him.

I grab Langston's gun from his hand and then quickly fire at Phin. He drops instantly to the ground.

Enzo turns quickly, shocked by the sudden loss of his enemy.

And then he spots me.

I figure he'll be angry for me interfering. He wanted to do this by himself. He wanted to prove he was worthy. That he was capable of winning by himself. To ensure he kept the power in this game. To prove to the voters he deserves to be Black over me. But I don't give a fuck what he thinks.

Instead of all those things, I see a bright grin on his face as he looks at me.

"That's my girl. She's back."

9

ENZO

I'VE NEVER WANTED Kai more than I want her now.

I'm dripping in blood and sweat. My shirt is torn in a dozen places. My jeans are scuffed, and I have several bullet wounds and cuts that need attending to, but none of that matters. It will never matter as much as Kai does.

Everyone else disappears in my world. The crew members judging us. The dead men lying on the floor. Langston. Liesel. None of them exist.

My vision is solely on Kai—the strongest fucking person I know.

I grin looking at how incredible she looks, standing with a gun in her hand after killing a man threatening to shoot me in the back. I was ready for the attack, I wouldn't have let him shoot me, but I appreciate the support from her all the same.

She won't apologize for killing him or for interfering in my fight. She won't apologize for looking stronger than me in the eyes of the crew watching, who will most likely vote her as their leader tomorrow. They would have already done it if they were smart.

Everything about her is strong—except her eyes. They soften for me. And I know. Her heart is stirring again, coming alive like a bear awakening from hibernation with unsure feet. It will take her a while to realize her heart is open again. That she feels things again. That she's vulnerable to loving me again.

For now, I won't push too hard. I don't want to scare her into closing her heart again. For now, she cares if I live or die, and it's enough. But soon she'll feel everything I feel. She'll love me as I love her. And for once, we will both be on the same page when it comes to our feelings for each other. And I can't wait to see how incredible that would feel.

I take the gun from Kai's hand and toss it gently to Langston.

And then I hold out my hand, begging her to take it.

She does, and I sigh into the touch.

She won't open up any more here. I need to get her alone. I tug on her hand as I race inside the yacht. I want to pull her into my bedroom, but settle on hers, figuring she will feel more comfortable there.

I know nothing is going to happen; I just need her alone and close.

Fuck, do I need her.

I slam the door too loudly behind her and flip the lock.

She jumps at the sound but doesn't release my hand. *That has to be a good sign, right?*

"Thank you for saving me," I say.

She bites her lip to keep from speaking. Probably because she would say more than she wants to admit.

Slowly, she pulls her hand out of mine, and I feel the loss of my soul. There is nothing that can fill it, only her.

"You're bleeding. You should call the doctor," she says, her words cold and calculated.

I won't let this end with her feeding me some bullshit excuse of why I should leave.

"I will when we are finished," I say, stepping into her space, pushing her just a little.

She retreats until her back is against the wall.

I sigh, and my hands land on the wall behind her, instead of grasping her like I want. I cage her in with my hands, our breathing mixing between us like a sweet perfume.

Her fingers move up in the empty space between us.

I stop breathing. My heart stops pumping. My eyes stop blinking. All that exists are her beautiful hands. I watch them, desperate to know what she is doing.

Gently, her thumb brushes against my bottom lip where I'm bleeding.

I can't decide between closing my eyes to soak up her touch or keep them open to soak up her look. Ultimately, I decide to keep them open, because I can't stand to not watch her every chance I get. It's the right decision, because I see her pain at feeling things for me.

My breathing starts again, slow and steaming, like a caged bull preparing to take an arena and buck off his rider. That's how I feel, ready to attack. Ready to go to war for this woman.

But my fighting abilities won't make her love me. Rushing her won't win her heart. I have to be patient. I have to help her heal and remind her that loving me is worth it. That even though I've hurt her, I know when both of our hearts are synched, when we both declare our love for each other at the same time, there is nothing that will stop us. That I will never hurt her or let any other man hurt her. That our connection will only amplify and that will be what keeps her safe.

I don't know how to prove that to her. She's been hurt so many times before, by me included. I understand she is leery of love. But love is what will save us in the end.

Her hand carefully retreats from my lip.

"A part of you still loves me," I say.

She blinks but doesn't say anything. She doesn't immediately say I'm wrong.

"I gave you part of my heart. And that part opened your heart to the idea of loving me again. I didn't understand the love you felt for me before. But I do now. You might think it's safer for you not to love me. But no matter how you fight your feelings, you will end up loving me. It's inevitable. You can't control your feelings any more than I can," I say.

Her eyes bleed with pain and sorrow at my words. There is some reason she's not telling me as to why she thinks she can't love me—why she is fighting this so strongly. Because having her wrapped between my arms, I can feel her heart beat for me. Her breaths are for me. It's taking all of both of our restraints to keep our bodies from colliding with each other.

Just tell me, stingray. I can help you, whatever it is.

"This kind of love never fades. It either grows into an unstoppable connection, or it rips us apart piece by piece as we fight it, taking everyone close to us down with us like a sinking ship. Stop fighting it, stingray."

Tears stream down her cheeks.

Fuck, I can't handle more tears.

I lean close to her, unable to stay away. Unable to tread slowly. And then my lips kiss her cold tears from her soft cheeks. Her eyes flutter at my touch.

So I kiss her other cheek, risking everything so my selfish lips can touch her skin as many times as she will let me.

As I move my lips to kiss her other cheek, her head tilts up, and I catch the corner of her lips instead.

I gasp into her lips at the sudden touch I've craved for weeks. I don't move. My hands stay on the wall, and my lips barely open to accept the kiss.

If this is all I ever get from her, I want this moment to last forever. Even if it isn't the perfect kiss. Even if our lips aren't aligned. The kiss is like a sucker punch to my core. Reminding me of how amazing she is, but how far I have to go to make her mine again.

We are both frozen. I will not be the first to pull away. She will have to pull away first. She will be the one to break the connection. Not me.

Her lips shift, and I wait for the break. I prepare my heart for the rip of the bandaid about to happen.

But her lips shift to mine as she moans quietly.

Fuck yes!

I can't help myself anymore. My resolve is gone, and I'm thinking with dick instead of my brain.

My tongue collides with hers as I push past her wet lips, barely escaping the wrath of her teeth as she nips at me. Punishing me for touching her and not giving her enough of what her body craves at the same time.

I feel high from the kiss as I put all my feelings into the kiss. I don't touch her with my hands; I don't let my body press against her; our only point of contact is our lips and tongue.

But she knows exactly how much I want her. Need her.

And her hungry kisses back tell me she's just as needy.

Fuck, fuck, fuck.

I don't know if I'm helping my cause or hurting it. *When this kiss ends will she realize what she's done? Will she go back to hating me? Or will this kiss force her heart open wider?*

I can't think about any of that now. All I can think is more, more, more.

I can't fuck her like I want. I can't touch her without scaring her off. So I do the only thing I can. I fuck her with my tongue.

And I watch her body open for me. Her lips spread wider. Her eyes glaze over from the heat of the kiss. Her tongue pulls me in deeper. Her nipples pebble beneath the fabric of her shirt. Her legs inch apart. Everything about her tells me she wants this. She wants me.

But it's not enough for her body to tell me. Not anymore. Not after what happened.

She has to tell me she wants more. I need to hear the words leave her throat. And more than anything, I need her to tell me she loves me again.

But from the rough purrs leaving her throat, I know she's incapable of speaking right now. So I'll have to settle for the most incredible fucking kiss. One that's going to leave my cock hard for days and my balls blue wishing for a release.

I won't give in to my desires. I'll wait forever for her. I won't even get myself off. That will be my punishment. But even if I tried to jerk off, it wouldn't matter. My cock would realize it's not her hand touching it.

My cock only hardens for her.

I can feel her kisses slow, and I know her brain is operating again, telling her how bad of an idea this all is.

I try to hold onto this moment and spread it longer. My tongue swirls in her mouth, pulling another delicious moan from deep in her core.

Don't stop, baby. Not yet, I'm not ready to let you go again.

But it does end.

I close my eyes just before it does, to hold the memory

of the kiss deep in the vault of my mind. It's one of the memories I never want to forget.

"I'm sorry," she says, ducking under my arm and running out the door.

My instinct is to chase her, but I know I can't. She deserves the freedom to choose. I've already chosen her, but she hasn't chosen me back. And I'll wait forever until she does.

10

KAI

THE KISS WAS WRONG, and oh so good.

It's been weeks since I've felt anything between my legs. I haven't had the desire to even touch myself. I haven't felt turned on since before the incident with Milo. I can't even bring myself to think the words to describe what he did. I won't let him have that power over me.

But one kiss from Enzo and everything returned. I'm a horn-dog. I want sex. I want my nipples squeezed, my clit teased, my pussy filled. I want Enzo.

I can't have him.

He'll hurt me.

He'll put the baby's life in danger.

We can't be together.

But my pussy disagrees. She doesn't see any reason why we can't fool around with a man who knows all the buttons to press on my body to get me off.

If it were just sex, then maybe I'd do it. But unfortunately, my heart is still hooked up to my pussy. And once Enzo gets his hands on me, my heart will fall—fast, and fully for a man who is dangerous to me.

The one kiss is all I get.

I have to stop more from happening.

But that kiss already did enough damage. I don't know if I have enough restraint to keep my hands off of Enzo. Or to stop his advances. He knows I'm weak right now, and I'm terrified of what will happen if I let him win back my heart.

I spend the rest of the day avoiding Enzo, which is easy enough. He gets stitches and medical care, and then he's off barking orders to all his men to prepare for the next inevitable attack.

That night I get in bed, knowing I will need Langston to keep me grounded more than ever. The knock comes at the door, but it's Enzo standing in my doorway, not Langston.

"Langston is working. He's gathering our allies to prepare for more attacks. I'll be right out here if you need me," Enzo says, reluctantly.

I know he wants to jump into my bed. But I won't invite that level of temptation into my life.

I nod, and he closes the door. I pull the covers over my head, knowing sleep won't come easily. I try fingering myself under the covers, but that gets me nowhere but frustrated. I'm nowhere near coming, and sleep isn't close either.

Fuck, what are you doing to me Enzo?

Enzo's right about my feelings. Even after everything Milo did, they aren't gone—not completely.

But that doesn't mean I can be weak and give into them.

I need to be strong. I stroke my stomach. Another life depends on me being strong.

———

ENZO KNOCKS on my door at six in the morning.

I've slept less than an hour.

I moan and put on a robe as I get out of the bed. I throw the door open with a grumpy snarl on my face. My hair is a nest of hair on top of my head; my face is covered in wrinkle marks from tossing and turning on the bed.

"What?" I snap, still frustrated from last night.

I look at Enzo. If it's possible, he looks worse than me. There are stitches under his eyes and on his shoulder from where the doctor fixed him up. He changed his clothes from yesterday, but his skin is turning purple and blue and red and angry from the beating he took yesterday. And from the swollenness of his eyes and the exhaustion all over his face, I know he didn't sleep much last night either.

"Archard called a meeting for the vote to happen. Apparently, it will be happening at the crack of dawn every day," he says, thrusting a cup of coffee into my hands.

I take it, my fingers brushing against his. The touch jolting us both awake more than any cup of coffee ever could.

"Thanks," I say, letting our fingers linger for longer than I should. I'm only giving him hope each time I touch him. *But maybe it's myself I'm fooling?*

He clears his throat, and I see his length pressing against his jeans from just the touch.

My insides melt at what I do to him.

No!

I shake my head and sip my coffee as I walk upstairs.

Archard has already assembled the team of people who will vote on who the next leader will be for today.

I yawn as I take a seat at the long table. Enzo takes a seat next to me.

"The vote will happen every day promptly at six,"

Archard says, glaring at Enzo and me for being five minutes late.

I roll my eyes and sip my coffee.

It's only after a few sips that I realize I don't know if I'm allowed to drink coffee or not. *Will the caffeine hurt the baby?*

I set the cup down, but I know I need the caffeine to stay awake today. I decide one cup can't be that bad. But I need to corner the doctor to ask. He's not an OBGYN, but I assume he has basic knowledge of what I am and am not allowed to consume while pregnant. When the chance arises, I'll make an appointment with a doctor who can give me better advice.

"Alright, let's get this started. You are all voting based on yesterday's performance who you think should lead the empire today—Enzo or Kai. The majority rules. But everyone will vote out-loud regardless, so Enzo and Kai understand where they stand with each of the judges," Archard says. He nods to the first person.

I already forgot all their names. I would make a seriously terrible leader.

"Enzo," the first man says.

"Enzo."

"Enzo."

The first three men all voted for Enzo. So he remains the leader. It doesn't surprise me. All I did yesterday was fire a gun to kill one man, while Enzo fought off an entire team of men trying to kill him.

"Enzo," the fourth man says, which leaves the lone woman.

"Enzo," she says.

The vote doesn't shock me. It's better that Enzo is the leader. I'm in less danger than if I were in charge. But some part of my ego is hurt just a little. *I wouldn't make that bad of a leader, would I?* And I did kill the man in charge of the attack yesterday. But I guess that's not enough to earn me a single vote.

Enzo's lips tighten, instead of turning smug like I expect as he stares down the five people that voted.

"Thank you, that ends the vote for today, you can all return to your usual tasks," Archard says.

But as soon as the words leave his mouth, gunfire erupts.

Enzo's eyes meet mine; this is what we were afraid was going to happen. Daily attacks to test the leader. From every enemy we've ever faced. They'll be relentless. They will attack daily for a month. A new attack and surprise every day.

This is the worst place for a pregnant woman to be. I need to go lock myself away somewhere or better yet, get off this yacht and away from Enzo. But something keeps me rooted next to Enzo.

He tosses me a gun, which I catch automatically. *Is he going to let me fight with him?*

"Go lock yourself in my bedroom. It's the most secure room on the yacht. And don't open the door for anyone," Enzo orders.

I frown.

"Go," he shouts again and then runs off to start giving orders as more guns are fired.

Fuck.

Okay, little one. You win. I'll keep you safe.

And I know as I head to Enzo's room to barricade myself how much I will never be able to put Enzo first in my life. This baby will always come first. Always. It's not fair to Enzo to love him. It's better if I hate him. And that's exactly what I plan on doing.

11

ENZO

THE DAYS PASS AS A BLUR, each worse than the previous one.

The morning starts with a six o'clock meeting that always ends with a unanimous vote in my favor. It's beginning to piss me off, because Kai is just as capable, if not better, at leading. But I guess I prefer it this way, it keeps her out of harm's way.

But that isn't the worst part. The hard part is the relentless attacks—every fucking day.

I will admit, I like fighting. I like the adrenaline pumping through me. I feel alive with a gun in my hand.

But I hate being separated from Kai. And with each day that passes, it seems we grow further apart instead of closer together again. And I can't stand it. I don't know what changed since that kiss, but something did. And I'm going to get us back on track, tonight.

I fire my gun again, wishing Langston had returned with more reinforcement. Not because I'm not strong enough to take on an army by myself, but because I need someone else to talk to. He might have an idea of how to get through to

Kai. Langston might have an idea of what is happening with Kai.

My last attacker falls.

Only three o'clock in the afternoon. I grin. I have hours until the next battle. Although, I'm guessing soon, my father will have arranged multiple attacks in a day. But it's only the first week, so hopefully, those won't kick in until the second or third.

I should thank my father for giving me an easy task to win, one that shows off my strengths. But I want to curse him because this task lasts so fucking long.

I just want this over. As soon as the game is over, then I can figure out a plan to keep Kai in my life.

My phone buzzes—Langston.

"Tell me you have good news."

"I do. I'll be back tomorrow, with reinforcements."

"Thank fuck."

"Miss me?"

"Something like that."

I end the call and then head toward my bedroom where Kai holes herself in during the assault. But I know when I open the door, she'll be her usually icy self again. And I can't wait to melt her shell.

I unlock the door with a complex code and key but know I need to up the security on this door if the raids are going to keep getting worse. I don't want to risk Kai's life every time my father sends another attack from the grave.

I usually knock to warn Kai before I open the door, but in my excitement and high adrenaline state to get to her, I forget. I throw open the door, desperate to ensure she is okay after our latest onslaught.

I find her lying in bed; the covers pulled lazily over her waist. Her eyelids are hooded; her cheeks flushed, her mouth parted with her tongue rubbing over her swollen lip. Her arm rests on her stomach, disappearing beneath the boxer shorts she's wearing poking out from the comforter.

Lust consumes me as I watch the scene in front of me. What I wouldn't give to replace her hand with mine. I would gladly chop off my own arm just to be able to make this beautiful woman come.

Kai doesn't notice me at first. She's too busy trying to get herself off.

And being the sick bastard I am, I don't tell her I'm here. This might be the only time I get to watch the sweet look of euphoria cross her face. She may never let me make her come again. And I want to hold onto this.

I stand frozen like a pervert watching a beautiful woman through a window. I have my own personal peep show lying in the bed in front of me. The only woman I've ever wanted but never knew I needed.

I never understood the difference between a need and a want. Not until Kai. Now I know. *I need Kai.* She is my everything. My reason for existing. My motivation for taking out our enemies. My purpose for becoming as strong and powerful as I can. Everything is for her.

Kai moans loudly as her fingers rub faster under her blanket.

Jesus.

I bite my fist to keep from moaning with her. She's so damn beautiful. Her hair is splayed out on the pillow like a fan. And her skin glows against the sheets.

There is something different about her. I can't quite place what it is. But I feel a different energy off her than before. For weeks, I haven't been able to feel anything from her without concentrating hard. But now, I can feel her again. And there is something new I can't figure out.

Physically, she looks the same. Her hair and body are the same. She still doesn't wear much makeup or dress up unless Liesel forces her to. But none of that matters. She will always be the most beautiful woman in the room to me. And somehow, the strength that oozes from her pores is more powerful than ever before.

She gasps and arches her back as she circles her clit with her fingers.

Instinctively, I take a step forward but stop myself. She's so lost in her own world that I could probably crawl into bed next to her and she wouldn't notice until she finished. But as desperate as I am to participate, I won't. If all I can get is watching her from afar, then that's what I'll do.

Her head rolls back against her pillow. She's getting close. So close.

I swallow the suffocating lump in my throat as I ball my hands into tighter fists. I need a release, and I resist the urge to pull my cock out and start jacking off right along with her. It's been too long since I've gotten off. But I don't have the desire if it's not with her. But now, my cock hardens, pushing roughly against the zipper of my jeans.

I close my eyes for a single second, trying to pause the moment long enough to get myself under control, but there is no calm to find. I'm desperate for Kai.

But I don't let myself move; I am a statue. I don't deserve to feel one happy moment of pleasure. I deserve to suffer in hell for all I've put Kai through. My only job now is to protect her with my life.

Her breathing picks up from lazy moans to quick pants. Her teeth bite down on her bottom lip, trying to stifle any impending scream about to rip through her body with her orgasm. One hand stays buried between her legs, but her other hand curls up under her tank top to grab her breast. I can just make out her dark nipple beneath the white tank top. She moans as flicks the bud with her fingers.

I wait for the most explosive orgasm of either of our lives. I don't care if watching her is wrong. It feels right. Like I was meant to be here in this moment to watch her.

She's so close. *Yes!* I moan silently, egging her on. Needing her to feel all the pleasure of the world.

Suddenly, the moment approaches. The orgasm hangs on the edge of her body, but it never comes.

I've brought her to orgasm enough times to know this was the moment. She did all the right things. Her body was responding. I can smell the wetness of her sex in the air. But no matter what she did, it never happened. She didn't come.

And I don't need a connection to her to be able to see the frustration on her face.

She spreads her arms and legs out like a star in the bed, completely exacerbated with her body. Her eyes are closed, and she pants hard, like she just finished running for her life.

"Is the attack over?" she says suddenly. She still hasn't opened her eyes. I'm surprised she knows I'm here.

"Yes," I say at the same time I clear my throat, so it comes out muffled and strained.

She sighs and sits up, pulling the covers over her waist as she does.

"When do you think the next raid will happen?" she asks, acting like I didn't just watch her almost come like a pervert. And like she isn't sexually frustrated as hell and needs a release more than I need to breathe.

I shrug. "Probably tomorrow. So far, there has only been one attack a day, but I know my father. Soon he will increase the attacks until all we are doing is fighting off enemies. I would also guess he has more up his sleeve than invasions; I just haven't figured out what yet."

She yawns and stretches her arms up in a high V above her body. "Well, you'll be ready for whatever attacks come our way. I have no doubt about that."

I nod, but I'm not thinking about what onslaughts are coming. Or how the hell I'm going to keep her safe. I'm thinking about how much my chest aches because she didn't get to come.

"When is the last time you made yourself come?" I ask.

Her eyes widen into large green orbs. I don't think she's going to answer me. We may have kissed, but she's made it clear she won't make a mistake like that again. She doesn't want me anymore.

"I haven't come since the night we were together."

I exhale all the air in my lungs in a furry, and it feels like a hurricane sized swell just left my body. The pain on her face at not being able to make herself come is one thing, but the emotion I feel is another. I'm in so much fucking pain. Because I can tell from the way she's looking at me, she's not sure she's going to be able to make herself come again. And that is not acceptable.

"Do you trust me?" I ask. *Fuck, why did I ask that?* Of course, she doesn't trust me. She doesn't love me. I'm one-half of her nightmares. She has a secret she won't tell me. And hearing her say she doesn't trust me will only drive the knife deeper into my heart.

"Yes," she breathes.

Wait...what?

"You trust me?" I ask again.

She nods. "I trust you."

"Why?" *I really can't help myself. I need to stop talking.*

"Because you are the only person who loves me. I trust

that you won't purposefully hurt me. You will do everything to protect me, even if it isn't enough."

My heart clenches at her words. *So true, yet so painful.*

"I want to show you something," I say.

I hold out my hand to her, not expecting her to take it. But she does. I pull her out of the bed. She's wearing my boxer shorts and a white tank top. Her hair hangs down in messy strands.

"Beautiful," I exhale.

She grins timidly. Like if she grins too much, she will let her guard down and do something she sees as stupid, like fall in love with me again.

If only it were that easy.

"Where are we going?" she asks.

"You have to trust me."

I don't tell her anything else. But I'm fulfilling a need both of us have. I'm doing the one thing I can do to fix it.

I pull out my phone and send off a few text messages, and then I pull her out into the hallway.

I've lived my life knowing an enemy could attack at any moment. I'm always ready, but letting Kai trust me with her life alerts me on a whole other level.

I will not let her get hurt. Not again.

Not when I should be showing her the beauty and pleasure of the world.

I sneak her through the ship, careful to hide her in the shadows when one of my crew get too close. I don't know who to trust anymore. And tonight is just about us.

I let Langston know he is to stop traveling and keep his eyes on the security footage at all times. And if he sees anything suspicious, he should alert me, but otherwise, handle everything himself. Kai and I need tonight to ourselves. Even if Kai doesn't realize it yet.

We make our way to the back of the yacht where a small boat waits.

Kai freezes when she sees it. And I don't think she is going to go with me without me explaining to her what we are doing first.

"Am I dressed alright?" she asks.

I smile and tuck a strand of hair behind her ear, sending shockwaves reverberating between our bodies.

We both gasp at the sudden shock. A feeling we haven't felt since before our lives were taken from us.

"No one will see you but me. You are dressed perfectly," I say.

She stands taller as if needing the confidence boost to trust me in this moment.

"Ready?" I ask.

She nods.

I hold her hand as I jump down on the small dingy boat. And then I hold out my other hand. She grips both of my hands with hers, even though she doesn't need me to climb down onto the boat. She's more than capable of doing it herself, but she lets me help her. It's a start.

Our relationship has been anything but healthy. Neither of us knows how to trust. Neither of us knows how to show our love. Neither of us knows how to not be selfish.

We still don't know how to have a healthy relationship with each other. And we are both so fucked up that if we survive this game, it would take us the rest of our lives to figure out how to heal from all the pain we've caused each other. Our pasts have fucked us up. We need a fresh start away from all of this, but unfortunately, I don't think this world will ever let us go.

Kai takes a seat on the small bench, still gripping one of

my hands as the electricity continues to spark back and forth between us.

This is what I've been searching for my entire life. And I'll do everything to get it back.

We speed off into the sunset, our hands connecting us in a way our hearts won't let us. There have been too many lies, too much pain, too much suffering because of each other for us to let it all go and just love each other. But the flickering of energy going between us gives me hope we can overcome all our past mistakes. That we can grow together. We can heal ourselves and each other. We can overcome the mistakes our fathers made and the suffering we have experienced. And we can have a future together rid of any evil.

As I drive the small boat closer to Miami, I can feel the tension in her body. Her hand grips mine tighter.

"Trust me," I whisper. There is nothing else I can say. Just trust me.

Our eyes meet, and I know she does.

I drive faster, wanting to show her what I have planned as fast as possible.

We reach a dock on the edge of the city, and I tie off the boat with rope before helping her out. A car is parked on the edge of the dock. It's only then I realize I didn't even let her put on shoes before I whisked her away. There aren't any people on this portion of the dock, but I don't want her walking barefoot.

"I trust you," she says when she sees the hesitation in my eyes.

I scoop her legs up silently as I cradle her and walk to the waiting car, begging my cock to calm the hell down. Nothing is happening. But having her so close does things to my body I can't control.

I put her in the passenger seat and then jump in the

front seat of the Escalade. The keys are already in the ignition. I had one of my men park it here for me. I didn't want Kai to have to interact with anyone but me tonight.

"Are we headed to your house?" Kai asks. I can feel the hope and anxiety of that possibility in her voice. So many things have happened in my house here. So much in our relationship changed there. Good and bad. But tonight isn't about the past. Tonight is about reminding her the future is only good. It's about her. Us.

"No."

"Oh."

"Good 'oh' or bad 'oh'?" I take her hand again and kiss the back of it.

She stills, shocked that I kissed her like that.

"Good," she says, surprising me. Her tight smile weakens into a softer one.

I grin. Tonight, I'm going to give her the only thing she should ever have to experience in this world—pleasure.

It takes twenty minutes to reach the club. This club is very different than Surrender, which was only for members of my organization and people we did business with. This club is for the city. It makes money in its own right. And it sells one thing—sex.

I stop at the back entrance. Kai pulls her hand from my grasp, and I immediately feel empty and cold. Kai's body temperature may run cold, but I never feel cold myself touching her. And I hate freezing now.

"I'm not dressed to go into a club," she whispers sadly, like otherwise, she would enter.

"Good thing we aren't going into a public club then. Tonight, we have our own private entrance. Our own private room. Our own private club."

I climb out and race around to her door. I open it and hold my hand out again, praying she will take it.

She does.

The jolt returns.

She looks at me, curiously. "Are you expecting to get laid tonight? Because I can't...I mean, I'm not ready...to you know."

I hate how scared she seems now. I hate the fear in her voice.

"Tonight isn't about that. I promise. Trust me."

She licks her lips and nods.

I hope I'm doing the right thing. I think I know exactly what she needs tonight, but now I'm hesitant. *Am I pushing her too hard?*

Hand in hand we walk into the building. No one greets us. Nothing but a dark hallway awaits us just as I planned.

She takes a deep breath as I lead her up a dark staircase to a closed door. I enter in a code, and the door unlocks.

We both take a deep breath. Both of us unsure of what comes next. Me—unsure if I'm doing the right thing. Her—not sure if she should trust me with any decision in her life.

I open the door. The room is just how I wanted it.

An oversized king bed sits in the center of the room, with light-colored linens and oversized pillows practically begging to be laid on. The lights are dimmed, and the room is lit mostly by the dozens of candles spread. There is a bottle of champagne chilling next to the bed, along with two glasses. Chocolate covered strawberries sit on a tray next to the champagne. The room is as romantic and relaxing as most spas.

"Wow, this is beautiful," Kai says, her eyes taking everything in.

I relax a little, but she still doesn't understand why I brought her here. And it has nothing to do with me.

She lets go of my hand and explores the bedsheets with her hand, running lazily over the silk fabric.

She takes a deep breath, and the sweet aroma of lavender fills her nostrils from the aromatherapy in the room.

She tucks her hair behind her ear nervously as she looks from me to the bed, not understanding what I want her to do.

"Relax, beautiful. Tonight isn't about me. It's about you. I'm not going to touch you," I say.

She nods, but a frown tugs at her lips.

"There is more to see," I say.

I walk over to the nightstand next to the circular bed.

I pull open the top drawer and wait for her to join me.

She moves next to me and peers into the drawer. A light giggle, followed by a huge blush crosses her cheeks as she eyes the assortment of vibrators and dildos in the drawer.

Carefully, she trains her eyes on me.

"I thought they might help," I say.

She nods, still blushing.

"I want you to heal. I want you to be able to come and feel pleasure again on your own terms. There is one more thing I arranged that might help." It also might be too much for her. But I want to show her all the things that could help her.

I lead her over to the large wall of blacked-out glass. I press a button and stare at her, already knowing what is behind the glass. I prefer to study her face as the one-way mirror appears.

Her lips part hungrily as she stares at the beautiful men and woman dancing with each other. Soon they will start making out and then fuck, progressing slowly through each step. It will either turn her on or be too much.

But from the expression of lust on her face, I think it's turning her on.

I kiss the palm of her hand gently, trying to savor her touch and the scent of sex still lingering on her fingers.

"You did all this for me?" she asks, hesitantly.

"I would do anything for you, Kai. Anything. But yes, when I saw you were struggling to make yourself come, I quickly texted and arranged anything that I could think of that could help you get yourself off. If there is anything else you need, just let me know. But otherwise..." my voice trails off. This is when I leave her alone. Let her explore her own body again. Find pleasure in whatever it is that she needs.

Safety.

Calmness.

Erotic dancers.

Vibrators.

Whatever it is, she should be able to find it here.

Kai's gaze has gone back to the dancers. I watch them for a moment. Two men are pampering a woman with kisses and slowly undressing her.

But the dancers aren't what is turning me on—Kai is.

When I look at her and I feel the heat zooming off her body, I harden. Everywhere.

From my grin, to my chest, to my cock. Everything hardens, wanting Kai more than anything.

But I don't get her.

I don't get to be selfish anymore.

"Just because you have nightmares about what happened, doesn't mean you will forever. Someday you will be able to be with a man again. Until then, you need a safe place to enjoy yourself again," I say, hoping that man she fucks someday will be me.

I stroke her face, and then I walk away toward the door.

"You are safe here, Kai. No one can get in. I'll be outside guarding the door. You are free to find your way to healing."

She looks from me to the men who have now removed all the clothes from the woman and are kissing her everywhere.

"Wait," Kai says, as I reach for the door handle.

I freeze. Unsure if she's pissed that I did this or if she needs something else.

"Milo took so much, but he also gave me the truth. I don't regret knowing the truth even though it cost me so much," she says.

I turn and look at her. Hating that she won't tell me what Milo told her. *What truths does she know but isn't telling me?* The key to winning back her love is knowing the truth, but I can't find out if she won't tell me.

"Don't let him take everything from you. It doesn't matter what he told you. You still have control over your own future. Your own heart. Anything he took from you, you can get back," I say.

She doesn't speak. She just stares into my soul as if she's trying to remember why she loved me in the first place after everything I've done. She shouldn't love me. I'm a cruel man.

"Enjoy your night, Kai." I turn the doorknob even though it's killing me to leave her alone. But she needs this, and I would give her the world to make her happy, watch her with another man if it was what she needed to heal. I need her to be happy.

Her sudden plea shocks me. "Stay."

12

KAI

Stay.

One word with so much power.

I realize immediately what Enzo did for me. He arranged the most romantic, erotic experience for me the second he realized I can't make myself come anymore.

As soon as I saw the room, the cage around my heart melted just a little. And a tiny part of my heart lit up, reminding me Enzo can be a good man. But more importantly, he's a man who loves me.

This one gesture isn't enough to make me love him again. It's not even enough to give him a second chance. My heart is still locked away, out of reach to him. And I want to keep it that way.

But that isn't the part of me making decisions tonight.

I need to come.

I need a release.

I need it to feel good to heal. To move past what Milo did. I thought I was healing that night with Enzo after Milo raped me. But it was too soon. All that did was confuse my nightmares.

The only way I'm going to heal now is moving past what Milo did. But I can't do it alone. As much as I wish I could get off with all the gadgets Enzo got for me, the hot men fucking the gorgeous woman, and the most romantic room I've ever been in, it's not enough.

I need Enzo.

He's the only man I've been with prior to Milo. Enzo knows my body better than I know it myself. What Milo did doesn't get to define my future.

I do.

Enzo's torn face, when I told him to stay, would have been enough to melt a normal woman's heart. But my heart has been through more than most women's have. I've been poor, abused, sold, stolen, raped, beaten. I've been in more dangerous situations than most people who join the army. I've suffered countless injuries.

Enzo caused half of the pain I experienced, but in the depths of my heart, I know I need him to heal. To come.

But as soon as I told him to stay, his entire demeanor changed. He's scared. Terrified of hurting me and causing me more damage.

Another icicle falls from my heart. At this rate I'll be telling him I love him by the end of the night.

But then I remember the precious cargo I'm carrying in my stomach. The baby who deserves better than what Enzo or I can give him or her.

I can never love Enzo. It would risk my child's life. Possibly our child, if it's not Milo's. If Enzo knew the truth, he wouldn't want me to fall in love with him either. I'm doing the right thing for both of us.

But tonight, I'm being selfish. Before I leave Enzo forever to protect my, maybe our, child, I need to heal. I need to feel like a woman again. And Enzo is the only way.

It will just be one night. Enzo can't tell I'm pregnant yet. I'm not showing, but my time is running out. I need to get the hell away from this world as soon as Enzo wins this final game. And I have to make sure my child is hidden, even if it means giving him or her up.

"Are you sure?" Enzo asks.

No, I'm not fucking sure. Am I strong enough to fuck Enzo and not fall in love with him again? I don't know. But I can't live my entire life being this broken. Enzo has healed me before; maybe he can do it again.

"Yes," I breathe, and my entire body says yes.

Enzo's entire body changes with that one word. He's no longer terrified. He's turned on. For the first time in weeks, he allows himself to feel.

I need to prepare myself for what is coming. I need to try to remain calm to keep the nightmares and flashbacks away. But then I look at Enzo, and I know I don't have to do anything. He will take care of all my needs.

"Thank fuck. You have no idea how badly I need you, Kai." He walks over to me but doesn't touch me. He lets the anticipation grow in my stomach.

"I'm taking control now. I know what you need, and I'll make you come so hard you will be forced to release the pain. But if you need me to stop, tell me and I will. Even if we are in the middle of something. If you start having a nightmare or flashback, you have to tell me. Understood?"

"Yes."

"Good."

My shoulders tense as Enzo circles behind me. I close my eyes, trying to block out any negative feelings with my eyelids.

But I know Enzo notices, even though we aren't as connected as we used to be. He knows everything about my body. He knows when I'm lying and when I'm telling the truth. He knows when I'm hiding a secret from him. One I'm beginning to want to tell him.

My hand instinctively goes to my still flat stomach. It has begun to feel full and tight. Soon there will be no hiding the bump. And that terrifies me.

"Watch them, Kai," Enzo purrs in a low, seductive voice into my ear.

I open my eyes, watching how the men turn the woman on. Their muscles flex for her. Their tongues dance over her skin, bringing her blood to the surface of her skin, and alerting her nerve endings to impending pleasure. The woman moans, and I feel an ache between my legs from the guttural sound.

"You deserve to be worshipped, beautiful."

Enzo's words brush against my neck with his breath, but he doesn't touch me.

One of the men licks over the woman's plump breasts, teasing and taunting her nipples to harden for him.

I feel my own nipples pebble, wanting to be licked like that.

The other man spreads the woman's legs apart. His mouth lowers between her legs, and his tongue licks around her slit, careful not to actually touch her clit. I watch as the woman writhes, arching her back, trying to get the man to lick the sensitive bud. But he won't. He enjoys tormenting her too much.

She wiggles harder, bucking, moaning, and screaming as the feelings become more and more intense.

"No," I say.

One of the men holds her arms down, while the other keeps her legs spread on the bed.

No, stop! Don't hurt her!

I run to the glass and start pounding. They have to stop hurting her! They can't force her to do anything.

My breathing speeds, and my heart is frantic. I have to get in and help her, like no one came to help me.

"Stop!" I scream. But they either can't hear me or don't care. They keep torturing the woman.

Suddenly, the glass goes dark. I can't see the woman or men anymore.

"No," I back away from the glass and start looking for a door. I turn and start running for the door we entered through and run smack into Enzo.

He doesn't say anything, but his arms wrap tightly around me as he holds me in place. I should feel trapped. His biceps are holding me so tightly, but I don't feel scared, I feel safe in his arms.

I huff loudly in his strong muscles. My panting slowing with each exhale. My heart flutters hard in my chest, but his is slow and steady, so I focus on matching my breathing and heartbeat to his.

"We have to help her," I whisper, even though as I say it the words no longer make sense to me.

"She's not in any danger, baby," Enzo says, his voice calm with an edge of sadness.

He rubs my back gently, his nails scratching my spine as he moves his fingers under my shirt to brush against my skin.

He presses a button on a remote, and the screen changes from black to the scene again. The woman isn't being held down any more, and I see the look of euphoria on her face as the men kiss and lick her body.

"She wants them, stingray."

I watch while Enzo holds me in his arms. He's right; the

woman isn't in any danger. I projected my own fears onto her.

"I'm sorry," Enzo says into my hair.

"Why?"

"Because this was a bad idea. You aren't ready yet. And I definitely shouldn't have arranged for them to fuck in front of you."

I don't answer; I just let Enzo comfort me in his arms. And I watch.

Quickly my fear changes to hot panting. My fear and lust are close together. Milo tied them together. I need to rip them apart. I shouldn't feel fear when I'm turned on.

But right now I don't feel fear, only excitement. Enzo may think there is no hope after my overreaction, but there is.

"Kiss me," I say.

Enzo's body hardens, but not in the good way. He thinks he needs to put up all his walls to prevent myself from losing control with me.

"Stingray, I don't think—"

"Kiss me," I say again before I lose my nerve. "You are right; I need this. I need to move past what Milo did. Now kiss me before I go into that room and have one of those men kiss me instead."

Provoking Enzo into kissing me works. I stumble backward as his lips devour mine. There is nothing hesitant about his kiss, nothing that says he would rather be kissing any other woman. The kiss is carnal and rough. My lips tingle with each touch of his, and when his tongue slips into my mouth, I gasp like I've never been kissed like this before.

Enzo's hand crawls up my spine, pulling my shirt up with his hand. He grabs my neck and pulls me deeper into his passionate kiss. My hands press against his hard chest. My fingers quickly grip onto his shirt and pull him to me.

The kiss does everything to my body. Turns me on. Takes out my fears. Floods me with pleasure. Spreads a fire through my body that burns out all the pain.

The kiss continues on and on. Each of us taking turns exploring each other's mouths again, like we are two teenagers making out for the first time. But there is nothing new about this. This kiss is like coming home. With every kiss, I remember every previous kiss. I remember how good each and every one felt.

Our first kiss—the spark that exploded.

The kiss when I realized I loved him—how my heart beat for him.

The kiss when I realized he could never love me back—how I fell apart.

The first kiss after Milo—hope that lifted me up.

This kiss envelopes all of those emotions, but takes them all to another level. Because with this kiss Enzo loves me.

Slowly, Enzo stops the kiss. Our foreheads touch, keeping our connection. "I love you, stingray. There will never be another. I will never kiss another. My heart will never bleed for anyone but you. You are my other half. When Milo hurt you, I knew I would never recover. I knew I had failed. I knew I would never forgive myself."

I may be fucked up, but Enzo is heartbroken. I feel his warm, salty tears flow from his eyes to my cheeks and then to my tongue as I lick the tears away.

"Milo took the only person I have ever cared about. I was stupid for not realizing I love you sooner. Maybe if I did, things would be different now. Maybe I wouldn't have lost you. Maybe instead of trying to heal you, I would be getting down on one knee right now with a ring worth a small country and proposing. Instead, I will spend the rest of my life suffering."

I grab both of his cheeks and kiss them, I've never wanted to take away his pain so badly. But I won't. I can't take his suffering away, all it would end up doing is putting new pain on him. If I told him about the baby, he'd assume it was Milo's and be even more upset that he let it happen.

And even if tell him the truth, I still can't love him.

"You can still heal us both," I say with hope in my eyes.

He sucks in a breath, knowing exactly what I want. He wants it too, although I can tell he feels selfish for wanting me. He doesn't think he deserves to get to have me even for a night.

He takes my hand gently and kisses it again as he's done dozens of times tonight. A jolt zooms through my body at the kiss. He feels it too. It's in his hungry eyes.

"Don't be gentle. Be the rough, dangerous man I fell in love with. Don't change for me. I can't give you hope that I will ever love you again. But don't try to be someone you are not to gain me back. The old me loved how brave, fearless, and naughty you are. I would never fall for a man who was gentle and tiptoed around my feelings. I want the fierce leader who takes control of everything and pushes me to fight back."

With each word, I see the Enzo I used to love returning. Almost like what would happen if the prince turned back into the beast. The thirst in his eyes return as his eyes darken. The claws seem to return to his hands. His throat thickens as a low warning growl consumes the room. And his mouth tightens ready to devour me.

My heart skips a beat.

Shit. What was that? It's just lust. I can't have anything deeper than that for him.

"I don't know how to give you anything less than everything, baby."

He grabs my hips and lifts me up as his mouth attacks mine again. All panic leaves as I get lost in his kiss. Being with Enzo leaves no room in my heart except for being with him.

He possesses everything when he kisses me—my body, my mind, even my heart. I might try to claim my heart back when we are finished, but for now, it's his.

We fall down on the fluffiest bed I've ever laid on, but it doesn't stop the pressure of Enzo's body from connecting with mine. I'll be bruised in the morning, but right now, I want to feel instead of walking on eggshells.

His hands sneak under my shirt and run over my bare belly as he kisses my neck. I can't focus. I can't think. My toes curl, and my back arches.

I love having his hands over my belly. And for a moment I let myself imagine the baby is his. That he knows the truth. That we can give up this world, get normal jobs, and go live in a cottage in the woods somewhere.

A tear rolls down my cheek. That will never happen. And I know the baby isn't Enzo's. Nothing good ever happens in my life. My life goes from bad to worse. I'm sure the baby is Milo's.

"Baby? What's wrong?" Enzo says, lazily rubbing his hand over my stomach.

This is all I'll ever get. Enzo doesn't get to be the father, even the stand-in father. He doesn't get to go with me to doctor appointments. He doesn't get to watch my stomach grow, my feet swell, and my boobs ache. He doesn't get to be there for the birth. He doesn't get to help me make the decisions about how to raise our child. He doesn't get to be there. Because even though Enzo may be the only man I could ever love, he's also the man who has brought too much danger into my life.

So this is all my child will ever get from the only father my child could ever know. His palm pressed against my stomach. Enzo showing me how much he loves me even though I can never show it back—this is it.

"Nothing is wrong; this is perfect."

I wipe my tears and Enzo returns to his hungry kisses, hesitantly at first, but then he slowly realizes I'm fine.

My shirt comes off. Then his.

My boxers inch down my hips, but other than kissing my lips and neck, Enzo hasn't moved any further south.

I watch as he reaches into the drawer next to the bed where the vibrators are and grabs one.

"I want you," I say, sternly.

He grins, like I just made his entire year with my words. "I know, baby. And you will have me. Every part of me you want is yours. But first, I want you to feel so good there is no possibility of the nightmares coming when I touch you."

He clicks the vibrator on. A low buzzing comes from it, and he touches it to my nipple. My bud immediately rises and aches beneath the dull buzz.

"Holy fu—" I throw my head back at the intense pleasure.

He grins against my lips as he moves the vibrator to the other one. "Fuck, you're so hot, baby."

"I want—" I can't finish as he rolls the vibrator down my stomach and between my legs.

I want Enzo. The vibrator is amazing. But it's not the same as Enzo.

His eyes light with mischievousness as he watches me

come unglued from the vibrator. My body is turned on so much as he teases my clit with the vibrator, turning it on then quickly turning it off.

I know I'm soaked. If he held the vibrator on five seconds longer, I would come. But he pushes me just to the edge and then stops.

"I want—"

"What do you want, baby? To come?"

Yes, I want to come. But not like this. Each time he gets me close, I want him more than the vibrator. He knew this is how I would feel. That I would be so turned on I couldn't think of anything other than him.

"I want—"

The vibrator pulses faster, faster, faster.

"Oh, God!" I moan unable to form words or thoughts or anything other than the jumbled mess falling from my lips.

He pulls the vibrator off my clit just as I'm about to explode.

I sit up until we are eye to eye.

Both of us are panting.

Both of us have energy flowing all around us.

Both of us are hanging on an edge. We can either fall together, or split in two different directions.

"What do you want, baby?" he holds the vibrator between my legs, but he doesn't let it touch me. He won't until I tell him what I want. This is my decision in every way. He may know what I want and need, but he won't give it to me without me begging him at every turn.

"Please," I pant, unable to say more.

He grabs my chin and pulls my swollen bottom lip into his mouth. He sucks so hard and deliciously. He tastes like everything I've been missing—mint, musk, and love.

Fuck the love. Loving him has only ended in both of us hurt.

But with his tongue in my mouth, he makes a good argument for loving him again.

"What do you want, baby?" he asks, again.

"You. Fuck, I want you. Not that damn vibrator."

He grins, like he just won a prize.

He tosses the vibrator to the floor, and then his head disappears between my thighs. He grips my bare ass, and his scruff brushes against the sensitive spot, before his tongue takes over.

"Oh my god!" I cry when his wet tongue takes control. *Why haven't we been fucking this entire time? How could I ever withhold this intense pleasure from myself? How could I let Milo take this feeling away from me?*

The vibrator may have reminded me my body is capable of coming, but Enzo's tongue alone is reminding me I'm not only capable, but I have a need deep inside only he can quench.

"Enzo...I'm going to...fuck!" I come on his tongue and everything changes.

I've heard the saying that one moment can change your life. I've had those moments. When Enzo decided to let me live instead of kill me like his father ordered. When my father sold me. When Enzo sold me. When Milo raped me. So many moments changed my life.

But this moment squashed every bad thing that has ever happened.

It released all of the oxytocin in my body. All the good feelings I've been holding in explode through my body, and I know I'll never be able to contain those feelings again.

Enzo senses it too, although he may not understand exactly what change has happened.

He slowly lifts himself from between my legs, staring at me intently as his shoulders slowly rise and fall.

He thinks I'm done; I got the orgasm I've been so desperate for. And he was more than happy to give me that gift, but he wants more. He doesn't realize I want more too.

I could end this now, and I wouldn't end up too hurt. I got what my body needed. I got my freedom back, my body back. But I still don't have Enzo back.

I could tell him to leave now. I could sleep and nothing would change between us tomorrow. I could keep hating him. But if this is the only night I get, I'm not leaving with any regrets.

"What do you want, baby?" he asks, with so much hope and desperation in his voice. His hand rests on my stomach, and his thumb traces the edge of my belly button.

"I already told you. I want you."

It takes 0.1 seconds for him to understand the meaning of my words.

And then we collide.

I grab his pants, ripping them down just before his already hard cock enters me.

I'm so slick and wet; our bodies meld easily. This is what has been missing. This is what Milo took, and I'm taking it back.

It's not love. *That's not what this is. Right?*

This is just an intense connection Enzo and I have always shared—that's all.

But as my legs wrap around his waist, my fingers dig into his back, his cock sinks deeper inside me, his hands tangle in my hair, our eyes lock, and our lips devour, I know this is so much more. I have no control over what we are. I used to think I loved Enzo. Then I hated him. But neither word accurately describes how I feel or what this is.

This is life. This is everything. Enzo is me, and I'm him. I can no sooner remove him from my life than I can remove a leg from my body.

The agony on his face tells me he feels it too, and he's terrified of losing it.

"You are so tight, baby. I've never felt anything like you. When I'm inside you, your entire body grabs onto me, refusing to ever let me go."

"It's because I don't want to let you go." *Even if I have to.*

His bottom lip twitches at the thought of letting me go. "I have to move." His voice is strangled, like he's been holding back.

"Don't hold back," I say.

"I can't. Not with you. Hold on, I'm about to show you why we are meant to be together, forever."

He thrusts—once.

And a wall comes crumbling down.

Fuck, this isn't good. Yet, it's so fucking good.

Another thrust. Pleasure washes over me in a wave of energy.

Another. And I'm his.

My hips buck back against his, and he plunges deeper, taking down walls, demons, ghosts, and pasts. And I know once this is over, we will start new. I don't know where we will stand after this, but it will be a fresh start.

I don't want any more lies.

I don't want to hide any more truths.

I want to tell Enzo everything, because I realize in this moment, the only way to save my child is with Enzo's help. All the bad happened because one of us was resisting our love. Right now, neither of us is. And it's like everything aligns. My body, brain, and heart. They all realize what was missing—us both loving each other at the same time.

Fuck the consequences. We can figure out how to keep the rules of the empire and keep ourselves safe. We can love each other and still compete to be the ruler.

The baby...

Enzo will love the baby as he loves me, even if it's not his.

God, everything is so messy.

But in this moment, it becomes clear.

"I want this moment to last forever, but fuck, you're so tight, I can't last," Enzo says, ambushing my lips.

I know exactly how he feels, because it's exactly how I feel.

I want to speak. To tell him this moment will last, even after we both come. I want this—us. I want to fuck him every night. I want to tell him I love him. I want to tell him about the baby that is his in every way that matters. I want to tell him everything Milo told me.

But I can't speak. All I can do is make love to Enzo whether he realizes that is what we are doing or not.

The thrusting continues longer than either of us should be able to last. And when the shockwaves come, nothing can prepare either of us for the flood of delicious pleasure.

The feeling pounds into us—hard and deep. We are flooded with love and tingling nerves as I come hard around his dick, and he explodes into the depths of my pussy.

I still can't speak as Enzo pulls himself out of me. I can't murmur a word as he cleans me off. I can't produce a syllable as he curls his body around me.

"I love you, stingray. Nothing will ever change that," Enzo breathes.

Forever passes until I can say the words. Enzo is snoring, so I know he won't hear them, but I need to say them.

"I love you too."

———

I RUN, *my feet flying beneath me. In the end, I won't be fast enough. Not to outrun them all. One of them will catch me. It doesn't matter who. They are all the same darkness.*

Justin and his crew are running, but they are the farthest behind. Threatening to finish the torture they started. This time the threats of rape won't stop at threats; they will take me.

Enzo's father is coming. Telling me his game will be the end of me. Saying I don't know what's coming, but the game will destroy me because only Enzo deserves to lead.

My own father chases me too. I'm not good enough to lead. He wants me to keep running, forever.

Milo is closest. He's the one I'm most scared of. I can't let him take away my love. I just got it back.

My arms feel heavy. It takes me a minute to realize why. I'm carrying a baby—a girl. Her hair is long, dark black like mine. Her eyes are blue-green like mine too. But her smile is all her father's—intense, brooding, and lighting up my world all at the same time, just like Enzo's.

The men are catching up to us. I have to run faster, harder. I won't let them hurt my baby girl.

But I can't carry her alone. I can't keep her from the darkness. I'm not enough to keep her safe.

I stumble.

They are going to catch us.

They are going to hurt her.

No, run faster!

I will not stop. I will give everything to keep her safe.

Go, go, go!

There is a light in the distance. A man is waiting for me. He holds out his hand. I take it, and suddenly we are running faster.
The three of us.
My baby girl, Enzo, and me. Together we are enough.

———

I WAKE UP IN A SWEAT. The dream was so intense, and I don't know if any of it means anything.

I grip my stomach. *Am I having a girl?*

Is Enzo the father?

Will the three of us be able to survive together?

Or will one of the ghosts that haunt us finally catch up to us?

I need to tell Enzo about my dream. About my feelings. The truth about everything.

I reach across the bed, expecting to find Enzo, but the bed is empty.

"Enzo?" I say into the dark room.

No response.

I throw the covers off me and find my shirt and boxer shorts on the floor. I put them on quickly, but I still feel naked.

I sigh, *why can't I even enjoy waking up in the morning with Enzo next to me?*

I realize he probably had to go back to arrive in time for the stupid meeting at six AM. *But why didn't he wake me up?*

Probably because I haven't slept in a month, and he wanted to make sure I got good sleep. I can't be mad at him for wanting to let me sleep when I'm exhausted.

But this feels like more than just letting me sleep. I have an unsettling feeling as I walk around the room searching for a note, a clue, anything that tells me where Enzo might be.

I can't even find a bathroom door. My only choice is to head back out the door we entered through even though I know it only leads to a dark hallway and then out the back of the building.

I open the door and see a man standing there. "Enzo?"

The man turns—Langston.

"I'm sorry, Enzo had to go. Felix had news of an impending attack coming and needed to speak to Enzo immediately. Enzo sent me to protect you and keep you here until the attack is over, so you don't get hurt," Langston says.

"Wait...did you say Felix? As in the Felix that worked for Milo?"

Langston nods slowly.

"Fuck, we have to go," I say, rushing past Langston.

Langston grabs my arm. "Hold on, where are you going?"

I pull my arm free. "We have to warn Enzo."

"Warn him about what?"

"Felix."

Langston frowns. "I thought Felix was an ally. He helped us get into Milo's house."

"He's not an ally. He's Milo's brother. He's Enzo's half-brother. I don't know what Felix is up to, but it's not good. Enzo killed Felix's half-brother, Pietro. Felix and Milo wanted revenge against Enzo. Felix isn't here to warn Enzo of an attack; he is the attack."

"Fuck." Langston pulls out his phone. It rings, but no one answers.

No! Felix doesn't get to take Enzo from me, not before I even got him back.

"We have to go," I say.

"No, I have to go. You stay here. It's safe here."

I shake my head. "Not happening. I'm coming."

"Kai, you should stay. The baby—"

"I love him, Langston. I'm coming."

Langston sighs, tosses me a pair of my jeans and sweatshirt from his backpack, hands me a gun, and then we are gone. I have no idea what we are about to face. Another danger to add to my growing list. My stomach clenches. This is exactly what I was trying to avoid. I can't choose between my baby and Enzo. I have to choose my baby. But I need to warn Enzo first. Then I can run somewhere safe.

13

ENZO

I LEAVE KAI ALONE, naked in the bed with a large, stupid grin on my face. My goal is to get back to the yacht and back into bed before she wakes up. It's early, only four in the morning, and Kai is sleeping hard, so it's definitely a possibility.

I still hate leaving her. Especially after everything that happened last night. I finally feel like we connected. She never said she loved me, but she didn't need to, I felt it.

We are finally both feeling the same thing for each other at the same time, and nothing is going to tear us apart. Not this time. This time we are going to go all the way, with rings, a white dress, and I do's.

All the obstacles left in our way no longer matter. One of us will win the stupid game and produce an heir. If the crew doesn't want one of us to lead because we don't have a child, then fine. I don't care about running an empire. All I care about is Kai.

When Langston told me Felix is here and wants to talk to me about potential threats, I got suspicious. Felix has helped me before, and we became something like friends when Milo held me captive, but it doesn't mean I trust Felix. We aren't close enough that he should be here offering his help to me now, not unless he wants something from me.

I pull up the security cameras as I drive over on the small boat to meet up with the yacht where Langston sent Felix to wait for me. Everything looks in order. Most of the men are asleep with just two awake on guard.

Felix is sitting on the main deck, sipping what looks like a beer as he flips through his phone.

Everything looks as it should be. But I've learned through doing this job long enough and growing up in this world that just because everything looks right, it doesn't mean it is. And my gut is sending warning signals left and right that this feels wrong.

I should be in bed with Kai. I should be feeling so elated that I can't imagine anything else except her. Instead, I'm freezing my ass off in the middle of the night, speeding away from the naked woman I love to meet a man who is most likely going to double-cross me.

Fuck my life.

Fuck it all. If I can find a way to get away from this world, I will. I want to spend the rest of my life fucking Kai in a bed. I don't need money, or fancy cars, or big houses, or fighting to make me happy. Just her.

I slow the engine of my boat as I approach my yacht. All of the warning bells are going off in my head, but I pretend I don't notice as I tie my boat off and climb the ladder up.

Click.

The familiar sound of a gun cocking behind me as soon as I step on deck tells me I was right about something being off. I should panic, I can feel the barrel of the gun against the base of my head. But the only thing I fear is losing Kai, nothing else compares. And if the man holding the gun wanted me dead, then I would be.

"What are you doing here, Felix?" I ask without moving.

"Taking what should have always belonged to me and my family."

"Are we going to talk face to face like men, or are you going to shoot me in the back like a coward?"

He chuckles, but it isn't a pleasant laugh. It's the kind from a tortured soul that no longer knows how to find joy anymore.

"Sit," he says.

I walk forward and take a seat in one of the lounge chairs I've sat in dozens of times. Most men like doing business in an office. I prefer putting men in a different element, and watching them squirm, see how they react. Doing business on the top deck of my yacht doesn't feel out of play, but unfortunately, Felix seems to have learned all the same tactics I have.

He takes a seat in the lounge chair opposite me, still gripping his gun, but it is no longer aimed at me. He picks up his beer with the other hand. His eyes nod toward the table next to me. There is a bottle of beer next to me.

I don't drink beer often; it seems like such a boys drink. When I drink, I want the alcohol to hit my system fast and strong. I don't waste calories on a drink that will take a dozen of to get me remotely drunk.

But this morning, I guess I'm drinking beer. I lift the bottle and take a swig.

"What do you want, Felix?"

"You always were the impatient one." He takes another swig. "Don't worry, we have all the time in the world. All of your team is currently tied up."

My eyes widen, and my nostrils flare.

He smirks. "Go ahead, look on your cameras."

I pull out my phone and pull up the security cameras again. This time, I see reality instead of what Felix wanted me to see. All of my team is tied up and handcuffed together in one of the bedrooms.

"Who came with you?" I ask.

"You think I need a team to take out yours? I was able to take out all dozen of your men without breaking a sweat."

I underestimated Felix. I know that now. I don't know what he's up to. I don't know why he helped me when I was Milo's captive, but I know it wasn't for my benefit.

"Who are you?"

Felix leans back with a smirk. "Ah, now you are asking the right question."

I wait. This is all one big game to him, and I'm not sure how to play it yet. Thank god I didn't wake Kai up. Langston is protecting her, and he won't let her leave until I tell him it's safe to bring her here.

"I'm Felix Black."

I choke on the beer in my mouth.

Felix grins, like his entire life has been leading to this moment, and my reaction fell right into his plan. I'm usually good at keeping a poker face, but I'm not prepared for this.

"Or Felix Rinaldi, if you prefer. I think Black has a better ring to it. And since our father always went by Black, and you go by Black, that's what me and my brothers have always gone by."

Brothers.

I have brothers—plural.

I always knew my father was an evil bastard. He was never kind to my mother. He was the reason she died in the end. But I never knew he fathered other children.

I was raised as an only child. I was told I was the only

option to follow in his footsteps and become Mr. Black, ruler of his empire. But I had brothers. There were other people in my family that could have carried some of the burden.

Instead, my father kept them a secret. But now that I examine Felix closer, I see the resemblance. The dark hair, tanned skin, crooked grin, dangerous eyes, tall, muscular body. I'm surprised I didn't question it before.

"Your mother?" I ask.

"She thought he was the love of her life. But he was a wild man who traveled often. She never gave up hope that he would decide to give up his other life for her and her sons." He shrugs. "She died when I was still a toddler."

"Who else?" I ask, needing to know how many other half-brothers I have.

"Milo."

Fuck, no.

My skin crawls at the thought of sharing DNA with that sick bastard. He raped the woman I love. Almost took her from me. But then I knew we shared some level of blood—shared a connection, a past. I just didn't realize we shared a father. It makes me hate Milo more.

"But then you killed him, didn't you?" Felix asks.

"No, I didn't kill him. But he deserved to die."

Felix raises an eyebrow. "That whore of a girlfriend of yours killed him?"

"Yes."

Felix sighs. "Milo deserved to die. He was reckless and doing a horrible job leading the men our father left to us."

"Father left you men? An empire?"

"Yes, it is nothing compared to what he left you. But he left us enough to get by."

"My father left you and Milo money, men, a small

empire?" repeating my question because I can't believe my father just gave him something I had to spend my entire life earning.

"Yes, our father left the three of us enough to battle against you if you ever stepped out of line."

"The three of you?"

"Oh, I didn't mention our youngest brother, did I?" Felix's eyes darken with a rage I've only ever seen on one other man—father. And I have no doubt now Felix is my brother.

I wait, because whatever Felix is about to say is going to hurt. I know it is.

"Pietro. You killed him. You met us all once before. We were teenagers. Our father told you to kill one of us to test you, and you did, without figuring out why."

Fuck.

I remember it. I've killed countless people on my father's behalf. None of them deserved to die. I learned to stop asking questions and just follow my father's orders. I vowed when I took over, I would never be like that. I would never kill an innocent person. And I've lived up to that promise.

I can see the rage in Felix at me killing our youngest brother. It makes me realize why Milo hated me so much. It all makes sense now.

"Milo came to avenge our brother's death. I'm not here to get revenge for my brother."

"Then, why are you here?"

"I'm here to fulfill a promise I made to our father."

I shake my head. "Haven't you learned you should never do anything for our father? He was an evil fucker who deserved to die."

"Maybe, but he was still blood. And I watched him build

an empire that if you continue to rule, you will destroy. You aren't strong enough to rule. You didn't kill our brother because you saw in your heart how weak he was and knew it needed to be done, you only did it because our father told you to—that's weakness."

"I was weak, but not like that. I was weak because I didn't stand up to our father and not kill an innocent boy."

Felix shakes his head. "Father always knew you weren't strong enough. You never had the spine to do what needed to be done. It was the same with Pietro. Which is why he had you eliminate him. Father always liked Milo and me the best. But he felt since you were the oldest, and the son of that whore of a wife of his, you deserved the first shot at ruling. We've given you a shot. And all you've done is run the company into the ground. Your profits are dwindling. You no longer sell women. You only sell weapons to those you feel are worthy and will use the weapons for good. You spend half your time rehabbing women and protecting them from getting sold. And the rest of the time you spend fucking that bitch."

"Leave Kai out of this!" I growl.

"You're weak," he spits. "Kai is your greatest weakness, just like your mother was your father's. He eventually realized his mistake and got rid of her."

"My mother was not a mistake."

"Kai is. She puts everyone in this company at risk. Get rid of her, and I'll let you rule. I won't ruin you. I won't kill you."

"You couldn't kill me if you tried."

Felix rolls his eyes. "How do you think I was able to sneak onto this yacht, dismantle your security system, so you saw what I wanted you to see, and tied up a dozen of your best men? Father taught me just like he taught you. He knew he needed spare heirs in case you weren't strong enough."

His words sink in. Milo was dangerous, but he didn't have the skills needed. He was strong, but his need for revenge got in the way.

Felix fooled us all.

Me.

Kai.

Langston.

We all thought Felix was on our side. And he took out a dozen of my best men. He would be a tough opponent. I don't know who would win.

"Give up Kai, and I'll let you live. I'll let you rule. I'll even join your side."

"Why do you care who sleeps in my bed?" Kai is so much more than just the woman who sleeps in my bed, but maybe if he doesn't realize that he won't care as much.

He laughs. "Don't try to fool me. You forget, I watched both you and Kai in that prison cell. You both lived and breathed for each other. I know Milo told Kai our true history to try and break you up. But I can already tell from the smug look on your face he failed to end your love for one another. Kai has already forgiven you and fallen back in love with you."

He speaks the truth, but there is no need to verify it.

"What did Milo tell Kai?"

"The truth."

"Which is?"

"That you can't love each other."

"Why?"

"Because love makes you weak. Our families have been fighting forever to be the strongest. It's an honor to rule this empire. If you fall in love with each other, there will be consequences—your death. And the death of any person you care about. I will not let you live if you don't give up Kai. You will put her first every time over this empire. You can choose some random whore to be in your bed, but not Kai Miller. She will never become Kai Black. She will never be allowed to be your wife."

That's what Milo told her. That I would be killed if she kept loving me. She had no incentive to heal—no reason to fall back in love with me after what he did.

"I'm sure Milo told Kai a story. This isn't the first time a Miller and a Rinaldi have fallen in love. It ended in their demise. The death of their child. They never recovered," Felix says.

I curse under my breath.

"All of those men and women that follow you? As soon as they realize you two love each other, they will come for you. They know the stories from the past. The fools that fell in love almost destroyed the empire for love. They won't let you and Kai do the same. I won't let you."

My anger erupts through my body. "This is ridiculous! Me loving Kai has nothing to do with whether I would be a good leader or not. You just want me gone you so you can make a claim for the throne."

Felix shrugs. "Maybe, but then I'm giving you an out. Give up the girl, and I'll back off. I'll ensure all the men your father charged with keeping you in line never come out of the shadows. You will be free to run the empire how you want. I'll serve you. We all will follow you wherever you lead us. But if you keep her, I'll make sure you never wake up again."

My father did this. He arranged this. He's controlling me even from the grave. Ensuring I stay cruel, dark, evil. He knew I would fall in love. He may not have anticipated me falling in love with Kai, but he knew I would. And he saw love as a weakness. That's why he killed my mother. He got rid of his own weakness, and he wants me to do the same with Kai.

"Honestly, I would prefer you don't give the whore up. I've always thought I would make a better leader," Felix sips his beer cockily.

"Who are you calling a whore?" Kai asks.

Fuck no.

My eyes train in the direction of the beautiful woman supposed to be asleep in bed, waiting for me to return. Not here. Not putting herself in danger.

Felix's jaw twitches for a second. He wasn't planning on Kai showing up. And does it appear he's more afraid of her than me?

Kai's eyes land on me. Her green beauties sending me warnings of Felix. *She knew, this whole time.* She knew Felix wasn't on our side. He's as evil as it comes.

She's better at reading people than I am. Too bad we can't convince everyone we would do a better job leading if we did it together. Her strengths are my weaknesses and vice versa. But everyone is right; we would always put each other first over the empire. Which makes us both the wrong people for the job. But Felix is no better.

I see Langston frowning, his gun aimed at Felix as he takes everything in. He was fooled by Felix too.

Felix just laughs at Langston. "Lower your gun, friend."

"No," Langston says.

"Lower your gun, or a dozen of your men die."

I snap back to Felix. "I thought you came alone."

"No, I took out your men alone. I never go anywhere alone."

Felix snaps his fingers and three of his men, heavily armed start parading my team out, still handcuffed in chains and ropes.

I stand, my nostrils flared, ready to go to war to protect the men and women who have always been loyal to me.

"I'm going to kill you for this, Felix. My team doesn't deserve to be treated like animals. Untie them. This is between you and me," I say.

"I will. When you tell them the truth," Felix says.

I frown.

Felix stands and steps forward. "For generations, a Miller and a Rinaldi have fought to become your leader. They have risked their lives playing a game that shows you the winner is worthy of leading you. Worthy of the technology that could wipe out entire countries. Worthy of controlling billions of dollars of assets. And for generations, it has worked. The Black empire has grown with each new generation and those who are loyal live incredible lives under their protection. Only one generation has ever threatened that system. Because they fell in love, they lost sight of what was important. They no longer put you all first." He turns to Kai and me. "They are making the same mistake. They made an announcement when they first got together that they got married. That was a farce, a test to see how you would all react. You failed to react then. But now, they are in love. They will put each other above you. Now you must act. You want the strongest person to lead you. Well, it's time they prove it to you."

Felix snaps his fingers, and his men begin untying my team members. I should run over to them and check and make sure they are all okay, but my instinct is to run to Kai, to protect her from my madman of a half-brother. Instead, I force myself to stay.

Felix disappears down the back ladder and reappears with a woman who looks awfully similar to Kai. She has long, dark hair, and her body is bruised and beaten.

I growl seeing a woman so hurt in Felix's grasp. He tosses the woman forward, and she falls to the ground.

"What are you doing?" my voice beams, and everyone's eyes are on me.

"Winning," Felix mouths, so only I notice.

This was never about ensuring I was the best leader. Felix just wants to be leader himself. And he's more dangerous than Milo ever was. He's smart. He's ruthless, heartless, and determined.

"Kill the woman," Felix says, taking out his gun and aiming it at Clifton. "Or I start killing your men."

I frown, not moving. For one, I will not be blackmailed. Two, Clifton can hold his own.

"Why?"

Felix laughs. "I'm threatening the life of one of your men, and you want to ask me why I want you to kill this woman? Some leader you are."

"My men know I won't be blackmailed. I won't kill someone innocent."

"She's not innocent."

The woman cries on the floor in front of me. "She is."

Felix fires, hitting Clifton in the chest.

Fuck.

Clifton drops to the ground. Felix aims his gun at the next man, while Clifton heaves on the ground.

"Kill her or I'll kill another of your men."

I growl. "I will not be threatened."

"Pussy. Being a leader is about putting your men first in the face of anything." Felix turns toward the remaining men. "If he won't kill a random woman to protect you, he sure as hell won't put you above the woman he loves."

All their eyes go from me to Kai. They know I love her. There is nothing I can do to hide it.

"What about now?" Felix asks, aiming the gun at Kai instead of my men.

I have the gun in my hand aimed at the woman before I even realize what I'm doing.

Felix laughs. "See! He would kill an innocent woman to protect Kai, just not to protect you."

Felix holds the gun loosely in his hand as he laughs at me for falling into his trap. I don't have to look at all of my team to know how pissed off they are that I didn't protect them. He just turned my entire team against me.

"Good thing Enzo isn't the only one who is fighting to be the leader," Kai says, and then she fires at Felix.

She hits his hand, knocking the gun loose. His eyebrows raise at her, as if he knew she was the one that could take him out, not me.

Fuck, why didn't I shoot him in the first place? Because he got in my head. Because as much as I hate him, he's my brother. The only family I have left. And maybe I feel like he deserves a chance to realize how my father corrupted him before I kill him. Maybe I feel remorse for killing Pietro.

Felix jumps over the side of the yacht along with his small team of men. Kai runs to the edge with her gun in her hand, but from her disappointed look, I know he's gone.

I stay frozen as a dozen eyes glare at me. My own team is pissed.

Kai takes matters into her own hands and runs to Clifton. She immediately applies pressure to the wound and starts barking orders for one of the men to call the doctor.

Odette looks at the surviving members who take part in the vote for the leadership position. "I think we should vote."

14

KAI

Vote.

Why the hell do they want to vote right now? A man's life hangs in the balance.

"We can vote on who is in charge later. Clifton just got shot. He needs all of our attention right now," I say.

The doctor arrives on the top deck and takes over, applying pressure to the chest wound. After a quick examination, I realize the injury isn't as bad as I first thought. Clifton will survive.

Odette looks from me to Enzo who is still standing frozen. I don't know why he's not acting. But I can tell Felix got under his skin. He told him the truth about the previous generations of failed lovers. About Felix being his brother, I'm sure. But I've never seen Enzo like this.

He looks terrified, in shock, unable to act.

The woman Felix threatened still cries on the ground. The men are all looking stunned at Felix's little show. The whole scene is a mess.

"Langston, get this woman somewhere safe," I bark.

He nods, scooping her up.

"Denziel, go check on the security footage. Get it back in our control and ensure Felix and his men are gone," I say.

He nods, running off.

"Vance, check to see if Felix's explosive threat is real."

I look at the remaining men. "The rest of you be on high alert. Felix could come back and launch an attack at any moment. Be ready to evacuate."

Odette looks from me to Enzo. "We need to vote."

"The vote can wait."

"No, it can't. Not if another attack is imminent."

I swallow hard. I'm not the person to lead if there is an attack. They are pissed Enzo put my life above theirs. I'm carrying a child I won't hesitate to trade all of their lives to save. They just don't realize it. They can't vote me their leader over Enzo.

"All those in favor of having Kai be the new leader, raise your hand," the woman says, raising her own hand.

Slowly, I watch as hand after hand goes up. More than just the four currently conscious that are part of making the decision. Every hand goes up.

Fuck, what did I do?

I feel sick to my stomach. I just reacted. I just protected myself, my baby, and Enzo. And in turn, I protected all of them.

And now my baby's life is even more at risk.

I glance over at Enzo who looks even more terrified, because he doesn't want me to be at risk either.

Slowly, Enzo walks over and kneels in front of me. I'm not sure he's helping his cause with the team at showing so much respect to me. "I will protect you at all costs," he whispers.

I stand tall, stern, and unmoving. I can't love him. I can't show them I love him. There will be a mutiny. They will kill us all and most likely let Felix lead them.

"You put all of their lives at risk, you deserve to be punished," I say to Enzo.

Enzo just bows his head. Locking him away will at least protect him until I figure out how to get the crew to care about him instead of me.

"Lock him in a bedroom," I tell Odette.

She nods and grabs Enzo to lead him down the stairs. Enzo gives me a concerned look. He doesn't want to leave me, but he has to. If he stays, he's putting us all at risk. He's already shown how much he loves me. I can't show how much I love him in return.

Enzo disappears and then it's me with a dozen eyes looking at me to keep them safe, when all I want to do is grab the first boat and get as far away as possible from all of them.

Denziel returns. "I've checked the security footage, Felix and his men left on a yacht. They were headed south."

I nod. "Thank you." Everyone continues to look at me, waiting for me to give more orders. "Everyone stay on high alert. Felix will be back. Maybe not today, but he will be back. And when he comes, we will be ready."

And then I head inside, away from all the prying eyes. I don't trust a single one of them, and I'm not sure why they trust me. It's in this moment I realize how easily a leader can be knocked from his thrown by his own people. They all love their jobs, but they risk their lives every day. They won't do that if they don't one hundred percent trust the person leading them. Enzo just lost their trust. I don't know how long I can hold onto it. And Felix is going to do everything he can to make us look bad, and him look good. So they will trust him instead of us.

I take a deep breath as I walk down the hallway to Enzo's bedroom, where I assume Odette locked him away. He's going to be pissed I had him locked up. But it was the only thing I could think of that would show I didn't love him like he loves me. The team needs to trust one of us, at least until we can show them how bad Felix is.

I unlock the door and then step into the bedroom.

Enzo is lying on top of the comforter with his arms stretched behind his head, and his legs crossed. He didn't bother taking off his shoes.

I don't know what I was expecting, but it wasn't this.

"Are you pissed?" I ask, as the door falls closed behind me.

"At you?"

I nod.

His lips thin, before the grin forms. "I'm not pissed that you make an incredible leader; strong, capable, and powerful."

"But you are pissed?"

Enzo swings his legs over the side of the bed and walks to me in one giant step, like two magnets being pulled together. But he stops himself short of slamming into my body.

"I'm pissed that Felix threatened your life. I'm pissed that I was foolish enough to trust Felix, when you could see his deception. I'm pissed that you ordered me to my room like a child instead of letting me stay to protect you. I'm pissed that I was this close to getting you to tell me you love me again, and that Felix ruined it for me," he says, moving his thumb and finger an inch apart.

He somehow moves closer, but he still doesn't touch me. His breath is on my lips, his eyes burning into mine.

"Am I right?"

I swallow down the lump. "About what?"

He exhales hard, frustrated with me. "You love me, Kai. You were going to admit it. But now you won't because Felix outed our love to the team. And you think you are putting ourselves and the team in danger if we admit that we love each other out loud."

Truth. But also, a little bit of a lie. I can't admit I love him because of the baby. If it were just us I had to worry about, I'd have admitted it in front of the entire team and fought anyone who threatened us with Enzo by my side.

I nod, knowing the more words I speak, the weaker I will become. I want to tell Enzo the truth. I want him to know my secret. I was planning on telling him, but now... now I need to think more strategically. I need to know we have a plan to get rid of Felix and keep the entire Black organization from turning on us.

Enzo shakes his head. "This close." He moves his thumb and finger an inch apart again. "This close. We are always this close to getting everything we've ever wanted. We were this close to happily ever after."

I chuckle. "You don't really believe that. We are always this close to happiness, and this far from getting everything we've ever loved ripped away from us. Maybe that's our love story, one in which we stupidly keep trying, even though the entire world is against us."

Enzo grabs a strand of my hair and rubs it between his thumb and fingers, entranced with the single glistening strand. And even though he's only touching my hair, I can feel it, like a jolt to my heart. "The entire world isn't against us, stingray. If anything, I would say we are our own worst enemies."

He's right. We've self-sabotaged our relationship so many times. But maybe it's because we both know deep down how this is going to end. And it's easier if we aren't together.

"You aren't going to tell me you love me?" Enzo asks.

"No."

"Even though it's the truth?"

I bite my lip as I choose my next words. Do I love Enzo? *Yes.* Did I always love him? *Yes and no.* I loved him before I should have. Even when he was being the biggest asshole, I knew he was a man I could love. A man who would choose me over everything else if I made him fall in love with me. And now that I have, I regret it. Because I put an entire empire of men and women at risk by making him choose me over them. They will never trust him again, not without him turning on me.

"The truth and lies don't matter. All that has ever mattered is winning. You need to focus on winning the game. That is your destiny, I'm just a distraction," I say.

Enzo growls with a deep frown etching lines all over his face. His face has reddened, and his eyes darken like a storm in the night. If he wasn't pissed at me before, he is now.

"I don't give a fuck about winning the game, Kai. I don't want the company. I want you!"

He doesn't touch me as he speaks. He's afraid he would hurt me if he touched me. And I'm scared if he were to touch me, the sparks flying off him would ignite the love inside me like a fire I will never be able to put out.

I love Enzo.

But it's not enough.

And it's not true until I speak the words.

I can love him in silence. I can feel the bond in quiet. I can help him win the game and regain the trust of his team. I can help him kill Felix. But I can't tell him, I love him.

Because if I love him out loud, he might put me above the team that depends on him, and I might put him above the safety of my baby. Neither of us can be selfish when we have other people who depend on us.

But I can tell from Enzo's rage flying around the room that he won't accept my silence. He needs me to speak. He needs me to love him. *Can't my heart beating for him be enough?*

"Truth or lie," I start.

Enzo pants heavily, his nostrils flaring like a raging bull, his growl deafening as he paces, trying to let go as he waits for me to speak. Finally, he halts to a stomp, his panting all that is left to show how pissed off he is.

"I've never ordered a drink from Starbucks," I say.

Enzo huffs, clearly not on board with this version of truth or lies. He'd prefer if I revealed my secret. Or if I told him I love him. But that's not what this is about. This is about breaking the tension. It's about revealing the stupid little things in our heart no one else knows. It's about connecting in a normal, human way instead of suffering the pain we've both been dealt.

"Truth," Enzo says, with an intense fury behind the single word.

I raise an eyebrow as I push into his space, but I don't touch him. Other than when Enzo touched a single strand of my hair, we haven't touched each other.

"You're losing your senses old man, because that was clearly a lie. Who in their right mind has never ordered a drink from Starbucks?" I ask, eyeing his shirt.

"I haven't."

"You've never ordered a drink from Starbucks?" my voice goes higher in disbelief as I speak.

"No. Why would I when I've grown up around constant butlers to get my drink for me?"

I roll my eyes. "You're missing out. There is something about ordering an overpriced drink in their cups that does something to you. Makes you feel important when they call out your name."

"I'll have to give it a try," he says, his gaze following my hungry one, staring at his black T-shirt like it's the enemy. I want it off. I want his hard chest. I want his tight abs. I want his thick arms wrapped around me.

Enzo smirks and then removes his shirt.

"What are you doing?" I ask.

"I lost. Clearly, I need to remove an item of clothing."

"We never agreed to any sort of bet."

He laughs. "Your eyes did."

Truth.

And then I'm drooling as I stare at his impossible abs. I want him to lose more. I want more items of clothing gone. I want to fuck him, even if we have to hide it from the world. Even if the team realizes I'm fucking him, it doesn't mean I love him. Or that he loves me. I can tell them it's purely physical, and because of the weird tension of the game, it means nothing.

"Truth or lies," Enzo starts. "I want you to remove your pants."

I smirk. *Too easy.* "Truth."

Enzo leans into my personal space. "Lie. I want you to remove your shirt. I want you to keep your pants and panties on until you are so soaked that when you have to get dressed again, you will have a constant reminder the rest of the day of how badly you want me. And you'll regret not telling me you love me."

Well, I walked right into that one. It's my turn to strip an item of clothing since I lost. He wants me to remove my shirt, but he knows that's not the type of girl I am. So I strip off my jeans.

He growls with a light grin. His eyes deepening with my defiance. He likes being in control, but he also likes it when I defy him.

"You'll pay for that."

I lick my lip. "I can't wait."

"Your turn, baby."

"Impatient?"

"Never, not when it comes to you. I want to savor every fucking moment. And I can last a lot longer than you. You will be begging for me to touch you by the end of this game. And then you will explode on my fingers before I even get my cock inside you."

I pout wanting to argue with him, but we both know he's right. And I won't apologize for wanting him.

"I used to do gymnastics as a kid," I say, deadpanned.

Enzo sucks in a breath at my admission.

"Truth."

I chuckle. "Lie, I never had the money to do gymnastics. But why is it every guy's dream the woman they are fucking is a gymnast? Does it really matter if I can throw my legs over my head when you fuck me?"

Enzo kicks off his shoes, which I assume is the item of clothing he's going to remove for losing, but he doesn't stop. He undoes his jeans, and they fall to the floor, until he's standing in just his boxers, his erection on full display and impatiently waiting for me to touch him.

"You forget, I've seen you with your legs flipped over your head. And yes, it's fucking sexy as hell."

I pant. *Fuck me,* I think. But we are in the middle of a

weird power play between us. And I won't give in. I won't be the one who folds first.

"I was enrolled in gymnastics as a kid," Enzo says.

I laugh. "Lie."

"Truth."

"No way!"

Enzo shrugs, takes a step back, and then casually does a backflip.

Holy fuck! How did I not know this?

My mouth has fallen open, and I'm drooling for real this time at this sexy man. I never knew I was so attracted to a man who could flip like that. But it's incredibly sexy to know Enzo knows how to move his body like that.

"My father enrolled me in karate, gymnastics, even ballet. He thought it was important for me to know how to move my body during fights. I only did gymnastics for two years, but I was pretty good at it."

I shake my head. So much I don't know about him. So much I want to know. I grab the hem of my shirt and slowly lift over my head.

Enzo gasps.

I'm afraid my belly has popped, and it's clear I'm pregnant. But when I lift the shirt off, I know that's not why he gasped. He just loves my body as much as I love his.

I'm standing in my bra and panties.

He's standing in his boxers.

We should stop this game.

We should fuck.

But making the first move feels like we would be surrendering to the other. I would be admitting I love him. He would be admitting he doesn't care if I say I love you back.

So neither of us make a move.

My next truth or lie comes from wanting to give Enzo

something. I can't say I love you, but I can clear up part of my feelings. "I hate you."

The room stills at my words. Enzo stops breathing, stops moving, and I swear his heart stops beating.

I stare at him, begging him to speak so I can tell him it's a lie. I no longer hate him.

But he takes his time.

"Truth," he finally says with a tick to his jaw.

The pain in that single world is too much. I shake my head. "That's a lie. I don't hate you, Enzo."

A slow grin spreads on his face. "I know, I just wanted to do this." He shoves his boxers down, freeing his enormous cock.

Fuck me. Please, fuck me.

He smirks at my reaction. I'm panting, drooling, and begging. *Don't give in! Not yet!* But if this game doesn't end in the next five seconds, I'm going to tackle him.

We both circle each other as we get closer, but still don't touch each other. So close, so far.

"I know the truth about why you won't say I love you," he whispers.

My face falls. *He knows my secret? He knows I'm pregnant? Did Langston or Liesel tell him?*

My eyes search the depths of his, trying to figure out the truth. *Does he know?*

"Lie," I say finally. He doesn't know. He just knows I'm hiding something.

His face drops in pain. He didn't know if it was a truth or lie. He was holding onto hope the only reason I won't say I love him is because of him and Felix. But it's not. It's because I'm pregnant and loving Enzo puts my child at risk.

The silence spreads between us. The pain consumes us. And our love fills us. Even if it is never spoken, it's there.

Taunting us with what we could be, if only our lives were different. If only, we were normal. If only, we weren't constantly in danger. If only...

"Why won't you tell me you love me, Kai?" Enzo finally speaks, giving me a chance to stop the secrets. To tell him the truth.

"If I told you the truth, I would have to let you go. You would make me run away. We couldn't be together. At least not with what we are currently facing, and I'm not ready to give you up yet."

15

ENZO

I'm not ready to give you up yet.

Her words burn into me. And they are exactly how I feel. I'm not ready to give her up yet either. I will never be ready to give her up. Ever.

And her secret could tear us apart.

If that's the truth, then I don't want to know it. I can live without knowing everything about her. As long as she's mine, I don't care.

Kai's afraid of losing the empire to Felix if we publicly show how much we love each other. And she thinks if she speaks it out loud to me, she won't be able to hide it around the team. I hate to tell her the team already thinks we love each other, and there is nothing she can do to change that. The only reason they voted her in, and me out, is because Felix forced me to choose her over them. And how fast she reacted on her feet. She can make as good, if not better, leader than I can. I just don't know if she wants the job or not.

None of that will stop me from showing her how much I need her now. How much I love her. If she doesn't want to say it—fine. But I will make it as hard as fucking possible for her to keep the words from falling off her swollen lips.

"I'm scared," Kai says, her voice trembling as she stands in front of me in nothing but her black bra and lace panties. She couldn't have chosen a more enticing outfit to seduce me if she tried.

"Why?" I breathe. The last time I fucked her, I thought I obliterated her demons. Maybe I was wrong. Maybe it wasn't as good for her as I thought.

"Because I want you more than I should. And every time I let myself feel anything for you, any time I let myself hope, we get ripped apart again a moment later."

She's right. The closer we get to each other, the harder the storm comes crashing through to break us apart.

I want to promise her it won't happen again. That no one can tear us apart permanently. That Felix can't do it. That no enemy can. That none of the company can. Nothing can hurt us again. But it would be a lie, and I don't want to lie to her. So I answer honestly.

"I'm scared too. But loving you is worth it, no matter the danger that follows. I love you. If I die tomorrow because I loved you today, then so be it. I wouldn't change my feelings for anything," I say, brushing my fingers to touch her pouty bottom lip.

The touch brings her alive. And her reaction tells me everything she won't say. She loves me too, and she doesn't regret anything either.

Slowly, she unhooks her bra, letting it drop to the floor, then she takes a step back as she slips out of her panties until I can see all of her.

"Show me how much you love me," she says.

I grab her neck, our mouths open and connect in a brutal kiss. She wants me to show her how much I love her, but I know from the second our lips touch that we won't be making love. We are both too charged for that. We are going to battle with our bodies just like we do during the games.

Her nails claw at my chest as our bodies collide together. Begging me for more of me than I'm already giving her.

I fist her hair, pulling her head back to break the hungry kisses that have turned into full on pants. I know from experience with her she is going to come quickly, explode before I've even had my fill of her.

"You will not come without my permission," I say sternly.

She whimpers defiantly in my grasp, her tongue licking her bottom lip as she begs me for more kisses without a word.

My eyes lock in like missiles on her lips.

"Don't act like you control me, you don't." She slips her fingers slowly over her breasts, rubbing each of them, taking her time while I still grasp her hair, giving her a stern look. But she continues her defiant movements, slipping her hand between her legs and rubbing herself viciously.

She moans at the touch of her fingers against her clit.

"Are you going to fuck me? Or am I going to come without you?" she asks, her eyelashes fluttering innocently at me.

There is nothing innocent about what she's doing. She's getting me riled up, on purpose.

I growl as I grab her hand, removing it from between her legs.

"This pussy is mine," I say, as I take her fingers in my mouth one by one and lick all her sweet juices from her fingers.

"Mine," I say again.

She grins. "Are you sure?"

"Yes," I hiss.

I grab both of her wrists in one hand as the other lingers on her hip. I walk her back to the bed, denying her the kisses she is begging for. My eyes devour her instead.

"Beg for me, baby," I say, as I push her back onto the bed.

Her legs spread immediately for me, and her hands start making their way back between her legs. I grab them, stopping her from touching herself again.

I give her a warning look. "Mine."

She cocks her head, seductively. "Then touch me already."

I growl. "I'm in control."

She shakes her head. "That has never been the truth. We both fight for control every chance we get. And you love it."

She's right. *I do.*

I grab her by the waist and swing her ass up across my lap as I sit on the edge of the bed—my hand, rubbing her bare ass slowly, taunting her.

"What are you doing?" she asks, her voice breathy.

"Punishing you for disobeying me."

"I never—"

I slap her ass.

She yelps, but I know from the heat of her voice she likes it as much as she hates is. As with everything else in our relationship.

"You disobeyed me. I told you to remove your shirt, and instead, you took your pants. I told you I would punish you, and I am. Do you want more?" I ask.

It takes her a moment to decide. "Yes."

I slap her other cheek, watching as the redness spreads. "Do you still want to disobey me?"

"Yes, every chance I get if this is the punishment."

I chuckle lightly, throwing her on her back onto the bed. I climb over her. Not touching her, just watching her.

She reaches out to touch me, but I grab her wrist.

"You want me?"

"Yes," she breathes.

I kiss her palm.

She squirms beneath me.

I glance down between her legs. She's soaked, swollen, and so ready for me. My girl is always ready for me. I've barely touched her, and if I lick between her legs, she will come. I want her to come; I want her to have all the pleasure in the world. But I'm selfish. I want her to come on my cock first. So I have to be careful where I touch her or she'll combust.

"What do you want, baby?"

She arches her back, trying to touch me, but I raise above her, not letting her until she's on the edge of coming without a touch.

"Your cock. Fuck me, please."

Her words undo me. I grab her hips and sink myself deep inside her in one stroke.

Our moans roar together with intense pleasure. This is worth living for. This is worth dying for.

I don't dare move inside her. I've already pushed too far, and my punishment is waiting for her to stretch and accommodate me. So I wait. Long torturous seconds pass.

Her eyes glisten with the fullness she is feeling.

Finally, she says, "Fuck me, Enzo."

I can't speak anymore. My cock does all the talking as I move one long stroke after another inside her.

Her hips meet my thrusts, and soon our tongues are tangling together again. I slow my strokes, our bodies no longer fighting. We don't speak words meant to torture each other.

We make love.

Our movements may be long and slow, but we've both dived into this feeling.

And then too quickly, I see all the familiar signs Kai is about to come. Her cheeks blush, her body clenches, and she tightens around me, ready to explode.

I want to come with her. So I move harder, faster inside her.

Together we come in the most beautiful expression of love. This is far better than hearing the words fall from her lips. She's crazy if she thinks we can fuck like this, and somehow pretend this never happened when we're around other people.

"You love me?" I ask, while she's still coming down from her high. My only chance of hearing the words is if I catch her off guard.

"I lo—" she stops herself and gives me a dirty look.

I flash her a dimpled smile. "It was worth a try."

I pull out of her, and she reaches out to me, feeling lost without me filling her.

I understand, it's how I feel.

"Don't worry, beautiful. I'm not done with you yet."

"What?" she gasps, as I spread her legs wider for me and flick my tongue between her legs.

"What are you do—"

Her words turn into a long moan.

I grin as I lick over her slit. "I love tasting myself inside you. It reminds me how much this is mine."

She blushes more at my words as I slide a finger in her, feeling more of my come mixing with hers.

We have so many problems facing us. Felix being our biggest problem at the moment. The second being that Kai is now the leader. She's winning the game. And I don't know if she wants that power or not. I like watching her in control, but it gives me a panic attack thinking how much more she is at risk of getting hurt. She's smart, strong, and knows how to shoot a gun. But that's not the same as fighting. She's only ever shot when she wasn't getting shot at. It's a whole other battle when bullets are being aimed at you.

But for now, I can bring her pleasure. For now, we are in our own little world. For now, I get to show her how much I love her.

16

———

KAI

I HEAR THE KNOCK, but I don't want it to be real. Enzo is still buried between my legs, promising to bring me another orgasm after making love to me a moment before. If I weren't already pregnant, what Enzo did would have probably done it. I haven't felt so much love pour into one fuck as I did with that one moment. And now his face is buried in my pussy with promises of more orgasms. And I want this orgasm. I want all the orgasms. I'm selfish that way.

"I'm coming," I shout at the door.

Enzo smirks. "Not yet, you aren't."

I grip the sheets. "Just keep licking."

I don't have to tell him twice. His tongue dances over my clit faster now that our time is almost up.

Almost there...

Another knock. Louder this time.

Ignore them, I tell myself.

"Kai? Are you in there?" Denziel's voice rings through.

I sigh and move to get up, but Enzo's hands hold me down.

"Enzo, I have to go answer that. They can't know we've been fucking," I hiss.

"You aren't going anywhere until you come again."

"But—"

He pushes another finger into me, hitting that delicious spot deep inside my cunt, and I forget why I want to answer the door. *Why would I ever leave this bedroom again?*

"Enzo!" I cry out too loudly, but right now, I don't care. Let them all know what Enzo is doing to me. Let them think I'm in love with him. Let Felix take over everything. All I care about right now is this orgasm.

"Yes!" I moan, biting down on my lip as I come on Enzo's fingers.

He smirks and finally lets go of me.

The knock rattles the door again.

Shit.

I jump up, throw my jeans and T-shirt on, purposefully leaving my bra and panties on the floor. I don't have time.

Thankfully, I always wear the scrunchie Zeke gave me on my wrist, so I tie my just fucked hair up.

Enzo, on the other hand, hasn't moved. He's still lying on the bed completely naked, not understanding the seriousness of his team realizing we are in fact together, in love, fucking, the whole shebang.

I hiss at him.

He laughs but gets the hint. He collects his clothes and heads to the bathroom before I open the door. Enzo and I really need to have a talk. He thinks his team is just punishing him for the minor indiscretion of choosing me over saving them. But it's more than that. I'm not sure he believes the story about what happened in previous generations. I don't care if he's grown up around these people his entire life. They can still turn on him if they think their way of life is being threatened.

"Sorry, I was just about to step into the shower," I say as I open the door to Denziel.

He looks from me to the bed behind me. The covers are crumpled, and the pillows are thrown around on the bed. Not to mention the smell of sex. *Who am I kidding?* They all know Enzo and I are fucking. I just need to go with the angle that he means nothing to me, and I mean nothing to him.

"What is it?" I ask.

"Now that you are in charge, there are some things we need you to handle."

His vagueness isn't reassuring.

"Okay, what do you need me to decide?"

His jaw twitches just the tiniest bit. "The doctor wants to take Clifton to the nearby hospital. He lost a lot of blood, and he wants to do a few x-rays to ensure everything is okay."

"Okay?" I ask, confused.

"You have to approve the transport of Clifton. Boat or helicopter?"

"Helicopter, he should get there as fast as possible."

"It's not an emergency."

"I don't care; we take care of our injured people. From now on, if anyone needs medical care while under my watch just send them. I don't care about the costs; my approval isn't necessary."

He smiles at my words.

Shit. Shouldn't I be making Enzo look better as a leader instead of myself? I don't want to win. I can't rule this empire and take care of my baby. It would be ridiculous.

"There is more," Denziel says, indicating for me to follow him.

I follow him upstairs to the main deck where a half-dozen of the team is mulling around. There are papers scattered on the table. None of these men have given me the time of day before, except Langston, who is standing in the corner looking mortified to see me still in charge.

Trust me, I'm mortified too. This can't be happening. I need to find a way to show that Enzo is the better leader fast, before another attack happens. I can't put my life at risk like this.

I give Langston a look that says, *help me.*

But he shrugs like he has no clue how to.

Ugh, this is ridiculous. Why can't I go back to being invisible to these people?

Langston's eyes turn from me to behind me, and I know without looking Enzo has arrived. But this time, when he enters the room, everyone ignores him. I've never seen his team ignore him. They worship him. They jump at the chance to gain his approval. One snap of his fingers and they jump into action for him. But now, not a single person in the room other than Langston looks at him. They show him zero respect. They act like he's invisible.

I decide I need a coffee if I'm going to make it through today. So I turn in the direction of the kitchen.

"Your coffee, ma'am," a man holds out an iced coffee exactly like I drink it.

"Um...thanks," I say, taking the cup from him.

"Can I get you anything else? We weren't sure what you eat for breakfast."

My stomach growls, giving my hunger away. I'm pregnant; I should eat. And then I remember I'm not sure if I should be drinking coffee. I decide one iced coffee probably won't hurt though and start sipping.

"An omelet with toast would be great, but I can fix it myself," I say.

The man shakes his head. "Be right back with your omelet."

"Thanks," I say, feeling like this entire interaction was strange. I look at Enzo seated at the table, eyeing the pieces of paper I'm sure I was brought up to discuss, but I have no clue what they are or what needs to happen.

Langston sits to Enzo's left. So I decide to take a seat next to Langston. No one would think that is strange. My heart aches to go sit next to Enzo, though. Being this far away from him is too far away.

"Should you be drinking that?" Langston whispers into my ear, as he eyes the drink.

"Yes? I don't know. I googled it, and some coffee isn't bad for the baby. But I really need to get in to see a doctor soon," I say.

He nods.

Enzo spots our exchange and frowns.

I stiffen and avert my eyes. *Do not look at him.* My stomach will do little flips, my heart will race, my cheeks will flush, I'll start drooling, and there will be no way that the entire ship won't realize we are in love.

"Here's your breakfast," Denziel says.

"Thank you," I say, digging into the food even though no one else is eating. All eyes are on me.

I'm about to speak when Archard enters. "It's time for the vote."

Vote. Maybe they are done punishing Enzo and will vote him back in.

"Since Clifton is at the hospital, I called him to get his vote. He voted for Kai."

"Kai."

"Kai."

"Kai."

"Kai."

All five of them voted for me. My eyes are wide; I'm sure I look like a deer in headlights instead of the strong, confident leader they are expecting me to be. *How could not one of them vote for Enzo?*

Archard nods. "Kai will remain in charge until tomorrow at six when the next vote occurs." He leaves and then all eyes are on me again.

"Um..." *Shit, stop saying um.* Actually, keep saying it because it makes me look incompetent, which is my job for the next twenty-four hours. "Um...so what's with all the papers?" *Yep, I sound like an idiot.*

Good.

"There is an insubordinate crew currently sailing off the shore of Cuba. They have gone rogue, stealing all the cash from the last security detail they ran. What would you like us to do?" one of the members ask.

Fuck. I glance over at Enzo, who is lightly drumming his fingers against the table with a smug smile on his lips. I know how he'd handle it. He'd send a team to have them all shot.

I can't give that order. I can't order men to die on the word of one employee. But I don't feel this is something I should fuck up in order to convince them to choose Enzo over me. Men's and women's lives are at stake.

"Send the closest team to go after them and bring them in," I answer.

It must be a good answer because he nods, grabs his phone, and disappears to make the call.

I can do this.

Easy.

But apparently, there is more to tackle than just the one question for the day. The next man grabs some of the papers and hands them to me. I stare blankly at the large sums of numbers on them.

Ten million.

Six million.

One point five billion!

Holy shit, does this organization have a lot of money.

"The books don't add up. I think someone has been padding the withdrawals and stealing from us," he says. He points to something on the page. "See here? The numbers don't add up."

I add the two closest numbers he's pointing to. They add up to equal the sum below it, so I'm not quite sure what he's getting at, but he seems very worked up about it. So me saying the two numbers clearly add up doesn't seem like the correct answer to give.

"Do you have any leads as to who could be doing this?" I ask.

"I have a general idea."

"Do you have any evidence?"

"No."

I toss the papers back to him. "Then get me some evidence."

He grabs them and then disappears.

I take a bite of my omelet. My stomach welcomes the food in.

But I feel another pair of eyes on me. I look up.

"Yes?" I ask Odette.

"A politician from New York hired us to install the best security system at his home and yacht and to protect him for events for the past month. He hasn't paid."

Shit. My eyes cut to Enzo, who is chuckling lightly to himself at the panic in my eyes. *He would off the politician too, wouldn't he?* To set an example, so our next clients ensure they pay.

"How much does he owe?"

"Twelve million."

Twelve million! For some security? That's crazy! How did I not know how much people pay us to protect them? Is our security system really that advanced compared to everyone else's?

Enzo's nails tap harder, watching the anxiety flow through my chest. *What should I do? Should I just let him off?* That would be fucking up for sure. They would have to choose Enzo over me at the next meeting for letting someone get away with stealing twelve million dollars for it. So I open my mouth to say just that, but instead I blurt, "Send someone to rough him up and send a message. But don't kill him. He still owes us twelve million dollars."

Odette smiles.

Enzo smirks.

Fuck, I'm turning into a ruthless leader just like him. And I don't want to admit it but giving an order like that does something to my body. I feel warmer, a wave of energy pushes through me, and I realize immediately what it is—power.

Another man steps forward to get his orders from me. And this time, I sit up straighter, ready to handle the decision.

"We have to decide what we do about Surrender. Do we rebuild on the same site? Do we use another club as our headquarters? What do you want us to do?"

My shoulders slump. Surrender is just another of our countless assets, but I know it had a personal connection to Enzo. To his father. Enzo should be the one making this decision, not me.

But this time when I glance over at Enzo, he tells me nothing. The smugness is gone, his lips thinned into a line, his eyes blank, his throat tight.

"I'm not ready to make that decision yet. Get me more details on the costs of rebuilding and other options in the city for the headquarters."

He nods and exits.

And then, I'm alone with Langston and Enzo.

I exhale heavily before shoveling more food into my mouth.

"When did you have the time to make decisions like that every day?" I ask, looking at Enzo.

He shrugs. "It's part of the job. I got used to it. Most of the men already know what my answer will be before they ask it. So most of it can be done over text, email, or phone. Which speaking of..." he reaches into his pocket and tosses me his phone.

"Why are you giving me your phone? I have my own."

"Because that phone has a dozen unanswered voice-mails, a hundred unresolved emails, and twenty frantic text messages for Black." He gives me a pointed look. "That's you."

"It shouldn't be," Langston says.

Enzo frowns, snapping his head to Langston. He thinks Langston is dissing my leadership skills, not trying to protect me.

"And why the hell not? She's amazing! And she wasn't even trying. Think of how incredible of a natural leader she will be when she actually tries," Enzo gets in Langston's face.

Langston ignores him, looking at me.

"Langston's right. I don't want the job. I'm not good at it. As soon as someone attacks with guns, I'll let them all down. I can make decisions from an office, but not in the heat of battle," I say.

Enzo growls, not liking any of my words. "Langston leave," Enzo orders.

"You aren't my boss at the moment. I only take orders from Kai," Langston says.

Both men's eyes cut to me.

"Tell him to leave, or I'll profess my love to you in front of the entire team," Enzo says, blackmailing me. If Enzo did that, no one on the team would ever let him lead again.

"Go," I tell Langston.

He huffs but leaves us alone.

"What do you want?" I ask as Enzo approaches me like a predator about to spring.

"Why don't you want to be Black?"

"Because I'm not the best for the job."

He laughs. "You've been fighting me for three rounds so far because you thought you were the right woman for the job. What changed?"

I suck in a breath. *Everything changed.* And I have another life to worry about; it's not just me anymore.

"I'm afraid. I don't want to die."

His eyes tighten into slits. He wasn't expecting that response. I've never been afraid of death before.

He tucks a strand of my hair behind my ear, sending chills down my neck.

"Langston and I will never let someone kill you. I can't

promise you won't get hurt, because, with this job, it's almost a requirement, but I will not let you die."

"I know."

His eyes search mine for the truth. And I need him to stop, or he'll find it.

"Why do you want me to be Black? Haven't you been working your entire life for this?"

"I have, but I'm not sure I want anything other than you. And if you are in control and happy, then that's what I want: you happy."

"I don't want to lead the Black organization."

"I don't believe you. You haven't even had the job long enough to know if you like it or not. But I saw the spark when you gave the orders. The power suits you; it gives you confidence. Unlike me, you won't ever let it go to your head."

He's right. I wouldn't. But I don't tell him that.

I suck in a breath as his body presses against mine—all hard and ready to take me on the table where the team was just sitting a moment before. A table where anyone could walk in and catch us.

"I want more time with you, stingray. I want you to figure out what makes you happy. And I think I make you happy. This job will make you happy. And if you win this round, that means you have to stay for one final round. Which means more time to convince you that you love me. That you should stay."

I put my hand on his hard chest, but I don't push away, even though I should.

"I can't stay."

"Why not?"

"Because I can't be Black. And you can't lead either if you're still in love with me. The team won't allow it."

"They just need time to adjust and realize it won't mean their lives are in danger."

I shake my head. He's so wrong about this. Felix is just as smart and cunning as Enzo. He may not have been raised by Enzo's father. But he shares the same blood, and he learned the same tactics. He fooled Enzo; he almost fooled me. And he will convince the team he's a better leader if we fall into his trap. I may not want to lead, but I don't want the billions of dollars, technology, and thousands of lives to fall into the hands of an evil monster.

Enzo strokes my face again, and I close my eyes, feeling his warmth. And before I realize what is happening, his lips are on mine and I'm wrapping my arms around his neck. I kiss him back, wrap my leg around his and grind against it.

The kiss is hot and intoxicating. I feel drunk on Enzo as I kiss him. My thoughts vanish, my worries fade. The moans leaving my throat are driving Enzo wild based on the way he's devouring my lips with his hard body pressing harder against me. He sets me on the table, spreading my legs as his body rests between them. I can feel his hard cock even between the two layers of jeans separating us.

I want him.

I want this.

I love him.

He starts kissing down my neck, finding every sweet delicious spot that makes my toes curl and my inhibitions leave.

His hand slides under my shirt, running it over my tight belly up to my sore breasts.

And my reality comes flashing back.

I'm pregnant.

And this is risking my baby's life.

I push against his chest hard.

"No," I say.

Enzo pants.

I pant in return.

Our eyes are filled with pain and torture.

He wants this.

I want this.

And for a single moment, I let our eyes fuck each other. I tell him how I want him to take me on the table. He shows me how he'd flip me over and take me from behind.

But then I close my eyes, and the images of us fucking are gone.

When I open them, I realize I need him gone.

"Go help the boy look at Surrender. It should be your decision anyway."

Enzo steps back, giving me a silent plea to let him stay.

"But what if another attack happens?" he asks.

"Langston will be here to protect me."

He nods. "Are you sure? I'd rather stay—"

"I gave you an order. I'm Black. You ensured that. Now go," I say, my voice trembling with power.

Enzo's jaw ticks, but he doesn't fight me. He leaves.

And I feel broken without him near.

I need a plan.

But instead, I spend most of my day sulking that I don't get to spend it near Enzo.

The team all comes back to the ship and surrounds me, waiting for orders. But I have no desire to boss any of them around. I just want a way out. And I don't see the answer.

A large crowd has gathered by afternoon. Everyone is on edge, thinking about the looming attack. I'm surprised it hasn't happened already.

"So what's the relationship between you and Enzo?" a random voice in the crowd says.

My ears perk up, because although I didn't see who spoke, the voice sounds very familiar.

All conversations in the room fall silent, and all eyes focus on me, waiting for an answer.

"We are both competing for the same job. We spend a lot of time together because of it, that's all," I say searching for the voice.

Langston makes his way over next to me. "Felix is here," I whisper into his ear.

His body tightens.

"Go find him," I say.

"I'm not leaving your side if Felix is here."

I tense not sure what to do. I could order Langston to go find Felix, but he's probably right to stay by my side.

"Bullshit!" Felix says in the crowd. My eyes search, but I can't find him. "We all see how you act together. You can't take your eyes off each other. You got married for goodness sake!"

"That was a fake marriage so I would have some authority in the company, people wouldn't question it, and our enemies wouldn't see us as weak while we compete in these games."

"It doesn't explain the sex then," he says.

"Just because we fuck doesn't mean we love each other. It doesn't mean we mean anything to each other."

"Prove it," Felix says.

I finally spot him. He's at the back of the crowd with a smug grin, darting quietly behind the scenes. I want to out him. To tell everyone he's a weasel trying to make his way to become leader himself. But I'm not sure they'd believe me. I've only been their leader for a day myself. This is a test. One Enzo's father set up. And I will pass it.

I fold my arms over my chest. Langston rests a hand on

my shoulder, trying to calm me down, but I don't need to be calmed down. I need to shut up the rumors about Enzo and me once and for all. Enzo may think the best way to protect our position in the company is to convince them us being together is a good thing. I disagree. It only takes one person to think it's a bad idea for us to be together to corrupt the entire group. Felix is proving the point right now.

"Enzo is nothing more than a good fuck to me. I don't love him. I don't care about him. He's my competition. And yes, he's good looking, and the only person here who understands my position. So yes, we hate fuck each other. And yes, Enzo didn't want me to die the other day. But it's not because he loves me, it's because he wants to win fair and square. And of course, us fucking has led to some level of feelings for each other. But it's not love. We would never put each other before all of you."

The crowd continues to stare, and I know I haven't convinced them yet. I need more.

"I'm a woman. I have needs. Enzo is a very attractive man." Several of the women in the crowd nod in agreement. "And I need an heir. I wasn't thinking when I was fucking Enzo that having his child wouldn't be the best way to get an heir. But I'd like to open up applications. If you want to fuck me, to help me produce an heir that would be worthy of this company, then step forward and tell me. I'll be waiting in my office for a man who thinks he's worthy of the job." My eyes shoot daggers into all of their eyes. Letting them know I will only take the best, the most qualified for the job.

What am I doing?

I don't want to fuck anyone other than Enzo. I don't want to have any man's child other than Enzo's. But I can tell my speech did the job. Everyone believes I don't love Enzo. So for now, it's a win.

"Make sure Felix finds his way into Enzo's bedroom," I tell Langston.

His jaw tightens, but he nods.

And then I walk quickly to Enzo's bedroom and wait.

A few minutes later, the door opens, and Langston has a gun pointed at a smiling Felix's head.

"Should I kill him?" Langston asks.

"No. We need to have a little chat, him and I. Guard the door, Langston," I say.

"But—"

"That's an order," I say, sterner than I mean.

Langston gives Felix a warning look. "I'll be right outside. And if I hear one single noise, I will come in here and shoot you dead. I won't wait for Kai's order."

Felix grins wider.

"He's unarmed," Langston says, before shutting the door, leaving Felix and me alone.

"Are you done playing games?" I ask.

"No, but that was some speech back there. I didn't think you had it in you. Men will be lining up soon for a chance to plant their seed in you."

I try not to look revolted at that thought, but I know I fail.

Felix looks pleased at my disgust.

"I always knew you were the stronger one. You would go to great lengths to protect Enzo. And even now, I have no doubt you would fuck a random man to keep Enzo safe."

"Maybe Enzo isn't the one I'm protecting." *Fuck, why did I say that?*

Felix looks at me curiously. "You're the smart one. You

didn't trust me from the start. You're the only one who didn't fall for my tricks."

"It's easy to spot the devil when he looks like a snake," I say.

He smirks. "It should be you and I competing to become Black. We are the strongest two."

"The correct two people are playing. But Enzo was always the one meant to be Black. He was born to be a leader. He is the only one of us capable of doing the job," I say.

"So little confidence in yourself," Felix reaches out to caress my face.

I slap his cheek.

He laughs as his face slowly turns back to face me. "There is the girl I met in the prison cell. The one who was determined to defeat my brother."

"What do you want, Felix? This isn't going to end well for you. No matter what you do, the men will never follow you. Not long term. They will eventually see you for the devil that you are."

He shrugs. "Maybe. Or maybe you are the only one who can see my true colors. I can see why both of my brothers have been so fascinated with you."

I growl. "And how did that turn out for the brother who decided I was his property? His to do what he wanted with? He's dead now."

Felix grins. "Yes, but he got what he wanted first, didn't he? You, my lovely, might be worth the cost. Even death to taste what is forbidden."

I pull out my gun and aim it at Felix. I will never be raped again. I will never let a man take from me again. And I don't need Langston or Enzo to prevent it from happening.

"I suggest you start thinking differently, before I shoot off your balls."

Felix just stretches his neck back and forth; the gun not even fazing him. "I like your threats. They're cute. But you can't threaten someone who has nothing to live for anymore. Yes, I would love to lead the Black empire, but I'd also settle for breaking up your love. Because even if one of you wins and you rule without the other, your lives will be miserable. Seems like a fair trade, since you killed Milo and Enzo killed Pietro."

I search his eyes, but I know his words are true. There is nothing that will make him stop. Only death. He wants to make us both suffer for hurting him.

"What else do you have planned? What's coming?"

"Like I would tell you. Where's the fun in that?"

Fuck, I need to tie him up and torture him to get the answers. I'm afraid if I kill him there will be some hidden booby trap we won't be prepared for. He's prepared for his death. Nothing will stop him from hurting Enzo and me.

"Lang—" I start to yell for Langston.

But Felix's words stop me. "Don't worry, sweetheart. I'm going to let you live, for now. I'm even going to let you win this round. Because I know what the final game is. And I can't wait to watch."

"What is the final game?" I beg, even though I know he won't answer.

"My money is on you winning the whole thing, that is if you are strong enough to fight for it," Felix says.

I'm stunned. I try to understand his words, but I can't decipher them. And before I can react, Felix has popped the window open and is jumping out. I fire the gun, but I already know it's too late.

Langston runs inside.

"He's gone," I say.

Langston runs to the window, aiming his gun out and he trying to get a look at where Felix went.

But before either of us can decide what to do an explosion rocks the boat. Langston grabs onto me, and my hand instinctively goes to my stomach, like my hand alone is enough to protect my baby.

Langston grabs Enzo's phone from my pocket and pulls up the security cameras. There is a large hole in the bottom of the yacht. Water is flowing in. Men are running around, guns drawn. Some look bloodied and injured. We are going to sink. Men are going to die. And I have no idea what to do. We are in the middle of the fucking ocean. Miles away from land. And I sent Enzo away. I can either lead and find a way out, or run away and leave the team to die.

I stroke my stomach one more time. I'm a horrible mother, and this baby isn't even here yet. *How am I supposed to protect my baby from danger when peril is all around me?*

By being a badass that takes out Felix and any other person standing in my way. If they all thought they saw me as a leader before, they have no idea what I'm capable of. They just pissed of momma bear. And I'm about to destroy every person that stands in the way of giving my child his happily ever after.

17

—————

ENZO

Why the hell did I give Kai my cell phone?

I realize my mistake as soon as I arrive at Surrender—the site that once contained the building I despised almost as much as my childhood home.

Now, I'm miles away from Kai with no way to contact her.

I spot Chad, surveying the damage and speaking with a construction manager about what it would cost to rebuild. Except there will be no rebuilding. At least not on this site. Not if I have anything to do with it.

I walk over to Chad. "I'll take it from here."

"Kai Black told me to get her the information about the cost of rebuilding here," Chad says, folding his arms across his chest, eyebrows raised in defiance.

A delicious simmering shoots through me when he calls Kai, Kai Black. I love hearing my last name following hers. I'm a caveman like that. But instead of dwelling on the nice feeling, I roll my eyes. He would have never defied me like this when I was his boss because he knew I'd dismiss him immediately.

"I said you are done here," I repeat, my voice deepening into the voice I only use when I mean business.

The boy doesn't back down. He has a spine, I'll give him that. But his spine is going to get him killed.

I grab him by the collar of his shirt. "You. Are. Done. Here."

"I don't take orders from you. I take them from Black. That's not you."

I sigh, I'm not going to get anywhere by trying to order him around, not unless I want to kill him. And I don't kill people who are innocent and loyal. He's loyal to Kai, so he gets to live.

I change my tactic. "Kai sent me to tell you she has another assignment for you. I will be taking over your assignment now."

He studies me, not sure he believes me. But I was once his boss, and he knows I could kill him here and now if I wanted to. Plus I never lied to my men if I could help it. They gave me their loyalty; I gave them my honesty. So he has no reason to believe I'm lying now.

"Fine," he says, looking from the contractor watching us back to me. I release him, and he starts to walk away.

"I need your cell phone as well," I say.

"What? Why?"

"My phone died, and I need to contact Ms. Black to let her know I took over the assignment and sent you back for a new one."

He frowns but hands over his phone and disappears.

"Are you ready to talk numbers? I don't have all day," the contractor says.

"One minute," I say, holding up my finger as I dial my cell. I have a strange inkling something isn't right with Kai. And I need to confirm she is fine.

Ring.

Ring.

Ring.

Finally, on the last ring, I hear her voice. "Chad? Are you still in Miami? If so, arrange for everyone to get a ship and get to my coordinates immediately. We are under attack." Her voice is so calm and strong. She was born to be a leader. She's my other half. We just need to prove to the company we are better off together than apart. Maybe generations ago they were too sexist to believe a woman could rule or that a man could lead without thinking with his dick instead of his head. But times have changed. We would make a great team.

"I'll be right there."

I hear her gasp at the sound of her voice.

"Is Langston at your side?" I ask, hating I'm so far away when danger struck. *Why the hell did I listen to her?* I should have stayed on that yacht. I knew another attack was coming.

"Yes, he's here. And he won't let anything happen to us."

The phone goes silent then.

Us?

Does she mean me and her? Or her and the crew? It doesn't matter. I'm on my way.

I drive to the docks in record time and grab the fastest speedboat I can find. I don't even think it's one of ours, but it doesn't matter. I just need to get to her. Now.

I drive to the last coordinates, and I see the smoke before I see the damage.

Fuck no.

This can't be happening. I've had too many nightmares of Kai's death. Too many times she has been taken from me. Sometimes due to my own stupidity. Sometimes because of how dangerous our life is. But this can't be happening.

As I approach, I realize most of the yacht is underwater; the part remaining is on fire. There are men and women swimming in the water. There are other yachts of ours approaching, trying to put the fire out and dragging injured crew out of the water.

The scene is organized chaos. And for a second, I can breathe a little easier. I just talked to her on the phone less than twenty minutes ago. She was calm and already taking action. She is the reason for the organization.

But my heart won't stop hurting until I see her. Until I can touch her with my own hands.

I carefully inch my speedboat closer to the sinking yacht. The only plus is I don't see any enemies attacking. This was a hit from afar, a bomb from the looks of it. And Kai was on the yacht when it happened.

Jesus Christ, this woman knows how to attract danger to her. And she knows how to stop my heart.

But then I see her, her hair blowing in the wind, her face covered in dirt, blood staining her shirt. She has a phone to one ear and alternates barking orders into it and the men who surround her. She's not afraid. Most people would be terrified in this moment. She doesn't know if another explosion is coming or not. She doesn't know if she is safe. Men will die all around her if she doesn't do something to help them. But that doesn't stop my girl. She takes the lead. She doesn't let the chaos or lurking danger stop her.

And I've never been prouder of her. I almost don't want to let her know I'm here. I just want to watch her in the shadows. Be the sniper watching over her and shooting any danger that approaches her. But of course, she feels me.

It takes her a second to scan the faces and boats approaching before she spots me.

I feel her take a deep breath when she sees me, and the tiniest of smiles touches the corner of her lip.

She may have been in complete control before, but now that I'm here, she's completely fearless.

I want to jump up on the yacht, throw her over my shoulder, and get her away from the danger. But I have a feeling that is part of what this entire situation is about.

I'm sure Felix is behind this. And that's exactly what he wants—to show my love for Kai.

I wink at her, letting her know I'm close if she needs me, and then I start pulling crew out of the water, loading up my speedboat before bringing them to the larger ships to safety. Each time I have to drive away from Kai, still on the sinking yacht, it kills me. But she's as safe there as anywhere else in these waters. She'll get off the yacht before it sinks. Even if that means heading into the water.

She has a great backstroke. She can swim as well as any competitive swimmer. She will be fine. I have to let her shine, even if it kills me.

I continue to keep myself busy, pulling my men out of the water and moving them to safety. Over and over, glancing over my shoulder at Kai as often as I can.

Get off the ship.

But then I see why she hasn't left. A man is trapped under some beams, and she is leading the effort to free him.

I dump the last of the men off on one of the yachts and head in her direction. The yacht is minutes away from sinking, and it appears they could use all the manpower they can get.

As I turn toward her, I hear the sound I've been most afraid of—another explosion.

The yacht explodes in front of my eyes.

Fire burns.

Smoke bursts in a large cloud.

Remains of the yacht drop into the ocean.

No.

No, no, no!

I can't catch my breath. My soul is sinking into the water along with the ship. There is no way she survived that unscathed.

I drive toward the smoke, hoping somehow she got off. That she's in the water somewhere.

She has to be alive.

I don't feel an intense loss. *I would feel her if she died, right?* I would know it immediately. I would probably drop dead right beside her; I would have no reason to keep living if she were dead.

That's the only thing giving me hope as I speed through black smoke. I have to slow down, afraid I might run her or Langston over in the water.

I see a body, face down in the water—Langston. I race to him and pull his limp body into the boat.

With one hard press against his chest, water expels from his lungs. "Where's Kai?" Langston asks.

I shake my head because I can't speak.

He jumps up, not acting like he almost died in an explosion. I know he needs a doctor to look at him. He could have internal injuries, but right now, we need to find Kai.

"Kai!" Langston shouts.

I'm thankful he can shout, because I've lost my voice.

Slowly we make our way through the wreckage, and with each second that passes and I don't see her, my panic rises.

This can't be the end.

Not like this.

We approach a small dingy boat. "I'm going to search on that boat. We can cover twice the ground that way," Langston says.

I nod, agreeing.

He hops on and then we both head in different directions.

Please God, let her live. I won't ask for anything but her life. Take mine instead, just not hers.

Faster I race. Needing to find her faster.

And then I see her, clinging to a life preserver in much the same way she was when I left her to swim to shore that first time I met her.

I dive into the water, needing my hands on her immediately, even though I can tell she's still alive.

"You're alive," I say, my breath weak at the sight of her. Her face is pale, covered in soot, her hair is drenched in water and blood from a cut on her head. But she's alive.

"So are you," she exhales, like she was as terrified as I was that I didn't survive.

I pull her into my arms and swim with my legs to get her back to the speedboat.

We both collapse onto the bottom of the boat with me still gripping her tightly in my arms.

"You're alive," Langston shouts over us.

Kai laughs. "People keep saying it like they are shocked."

I kiss her forehead probably too hard, but I don't care. I just need to keep reminding myself she is alive.

"What do you want me to do, boss?" Langston says to Kai.

I look at her. I need time alone with her. And from her heavy eyes, I know she needs the same. She just nods at me to talk, exhausted in my arms.

"Get everyone medical care as fast as possible. Yourself included. And then get everyone in attack formation on all of our best ships. We are going on the offensive as soon as the team has healed and recovered," I say.

Kai nods her agreement.

"Don't take too long," Langston says, warning us. "And make sure she sees a doctor too."

I kiss her head again. "I will."

Then Langston leaves us.

I sit up, pulling Kai onto my lap as I start the engine again.

"Where are we going?" she asks.

"Away," is all I answer. Because it's the truth. I need to take her to a doctor soon, and I will, but sometimes the best medicine is just being with the person you love.

She leans her head against my chest as I drive us away from the wreckage and the people who depend on us for our safety. We did our jobs; we rescued them from the danger. And we will form a plan to keep the attacks from happening again. But right now, this is about us.

After riding several miles into the middle of nowhere, I cut the engine.

Kai sits up in my lap. And I grab her legs until she is straddling me on the captain's seat.

And then the tears fall.

Her tears turn to sobs. And I hold her as tightly as I can, wishing I could take them all away.

"I thought you were dead," she sobs.

"I thought you were dead, too."

"Never leave me again," she says.

"Never. I'm yours, forever."

Her head lifts from my tear-soaked shoulder. We are both dripping wet with saltwater and blood.

The cut on her head spills more blood. *Shit. What was I thinking?* I really need to get her to a doctor as fast as possible.

"Make love to me," Kai says, lifting her shirt and revealing her bare breasts.

Fuck me.

I need to think with my head. I need to get her to the doctor. But I know she won't let me, not until I've had her.

I nod, my eyes big, my throat dry, suddenly unable to speak.

Then her hands are grabbing my shirt and lifting it off me, discarding it on the floor of the boat.

I'm eye level with her nipples, and so that is where I start. I take the first bud into my mouth, my tongue taking its time tasting and seeing how she reacts. If she shows one sign of a concussion or—

Her moan sends chills through my body. Her hand clasps down on my hair, and her urgent lust is obvious.

My greedy mouth moves from her first nipple to her second. Her back arches, and she throws her head back until I can feel the wet mane of her hair dripping down her bare back.

So fucking sexy.

I move my hands to massage her breasts while I kiss up her swollen breasts and to her neck. Her tits fill my hands more than usual. *Did they grow?*

She bites her lip, and I forget about her breasts. I want her lip. I want her tongue. I want her biting my lip.

My mouth hungrily kisses hers. So incredibly good. Her mouth tastes good, even though it tastes like saltwater, sweat, and blood. None of that matters because I'm getting to kiss her swollen lips.

"Make love to me," she purrs into my mouth.

Love, she says it again. She still hasn't said she loves me, but hearing the word is enough for now. And I plan on doing just that.

I stand up, and her legs wrap around me. There is a small bench in the back of the boat. That will have to do.

I carefully lay her down on the bench, and then I undo her jeans before pulling them from her body. She shivers. I'm not sure if it's because she is cold, or she loves my heated stare on her naked body.

I quickly remove my own jeans, and the loving gaze I get back is worth everything.

I move quickly, covering her body with mine. To keep her warm, and because I'm desperate to be inside her. Our lips meld together in quick, sweet kisses. Her legs spread wider as my body presses between them.

"Enzo, make love to me."

And so I do. My cock slips into her wet body. I've never been so welcome inside her before.

Our eyes lock. Our lips stop as our bodies sync together, just breathing into each other's mouth.

"I love you, Kai." I kiss her hard as I rock into her, feeling the full depths of her body.

She kisses me back, but then quickly breaks the kiss.

"What?" I ask, pouting and demanding with my eyes that she gets her plump lips back on mine immediately.

She laughs. "I have something to tell you."

I groan as I rock into her again. "Well, tell me so I can kiss you again."

She bites her lip and blushes.

She's so fucking adorable.

"I love you too, Enzo."

I stop.

I don't thrust.

I stop trying to kiss her.

My entire world stops.

I'm sure my heart stopped.

The only part of me that moves is my ears. I don't trust my own damn ears. *Did she really say she loves me?* They move closer to her mouth, trying to listen to see if she will say it again.

She gets the hint, grabs my neck to pull my ear right against her lip, and then says, "I love you, Enzo."

I quickly look her in the eye, not trusting my own ears even though I heard her say it twice.

She smiles brightly nodding. "I love y-," she says again.

And this time, I don't let her finish. My lips slam on her as I thrust hard inside of her.

And then we make love—for real. We fuck slowly as the small boat rocks with the waves. And I can't think of a more perfect place for us both to say I love you to each other except on the ocean with us both pleading after barely surviving danger.

I feel her orgasm coming, and I hate that it's happening, because I know this has to stop.

Sensing it, she says, "I love you." As her pussy grasps my cock with pulsating contractions.

And I remember this isn't the end, this is the beginning. Sure, I need to take her to the doctor immediately after this. But she loves me. No one can take that away again.

Her orgasm knocks me into one of my own. And I fill her with my cum.

"I love you too, stingray."

———

I TAKE Kai to the hospital despite her protests that she is

okay. But when the nurse wheels her back for tests, she tells me to go check on the team. She says she's fine, and I can come back in twenty minutes when the test is done. That I need to show my face in front of the team. Show them I put them first. That they need a leader like me.

I don't argue, because they need a leader like her too. Our team would be stupid not to see how good we would make as a team together.

I walk the hallways, looking for members of my team to check on, albeit reluctantly.

Clifton is the first room I come to. He looks well; I'm surprised he hasn't been released yet. So I duck inside, deciding to test my theory.

"How are you holding up?" I ask.

"Better than the rest of the team. I'm lucky the docs hadn't released me yet when the attack happened."

"Don't worry, we are going to get the bastard who did this."

He nods with a smile, "I know we will."

"I have a question for you, Clifton."

He sits up higher in the bed. "Okay, shoot."

"Would there be an objection to Kai and I running the Black organization together?"

He stills for a moment. "Yes."

"Why?"

"Because we wouldn't trust that you would put us first."

"But can't you see we are better leaders together? We play off each other strengths and weaknesses."

He shakes his head. "When people love each other, it's not all flowers and chocolates. Couples fight, they bicker. They disagree. And they put each other first."

I frown.

"I like you, Enzo. I still think you would make a better

leader than Kai, but right now, you are letting your feelings show too much. You love her, but I don't think she loves you back."

"Why do you say that?"

"Just something she said earlier to the team that Vance told me about."

I frown. I will have to talk to her later because it's clear he won't tell me.

"You have to let her go if you want to be the leader, because right now, Kai would have to fuck up really bad for you to have a chance at being Black again. The only way to get your job back is to stop loving Kai."

Stop loving Kai? Not possible. If this is how the team feels, then I guess I'm out of a job. Because there is nothing that could make me stop loving her.

KAI

I said I love you.

I swore I'd never say those words again. At least, not to Enzo.

But I said them.

And I don't regret it.

The words may end up being a mistake. But I would never take them back. That moment with Enzo on the speedboat was one of the purest experiences of my life. I felt everything we said and did. And if that moment is my downfall, then so be it.

"Would you like to hear your baby's heartbeat?" the doctor asks.

I nod.

The doctors told me the baby is fine. The cuts and bruises were minor, and the smoke inhalation shouldn't have any lasting effects. But I'm not sure I believe them. Not until I have some sort of proof.

The doctor said I could also have an ultrasound done if I want, but I don't want one. That seems like something Enzo should be here for. And if they showed me the baby on an ultrasound, I'd want a picture. I'd have physical evidence of my pregnancy. Which would only put the baby at risk.

But no harm can come from hearing the baby's heartbeat.

I lift my shirt up. My stomach still hasn't popped yet, but the doctor told me it would happen soon. One day I will wake up and have a belly that wasn't there when I went to sleep.

She puts the small device to my stomach.

Thump-thump.

Thump-thump.

Thump-thump.

She grins at me, and I know what I'm listening to: the perfect, magical sound of my baby's heartbeat. I'm in love. Sure, I love Enzo, but this... this is different. This is a love that can never be severed. This feeling encompasses all that I am. It's in my blood. No matter what happens, I will never be able to stop loving this child.

For just a second, the woman's smile changes, and quickly moves from her normal grin to a more knowing gleam.

"What?" I ask.

But as I ask the question I'm desperate to know the answer to, Enzo pops his head in.

I quickly brush the machine off my stomach, stopping the beautiful melody of my child's heartbeat.

The doctor catches on quickly and doesn't say anything about the baby.

I want to tell Enzo.

I don't want to tell him.

I have no clue how to protect my child.

But I absolutely don't want to tell him in a doctor's office where our employees reside in beds just next door.

Enzo looks from me to the doctor. "Is everything okay?" His voice cracks as he speaks, and I can tell now how hard it was for him to leave me.

"Yep, I'm completely healthy," I say.

Enzo looks from me to the doctor, waiting for her response. "If she needs to take it easy the next couple of days, stay in bed, then tell me. I'll make sure she follows my orders."

"No need, Miss Miller is completely healthy, albeit a little beat up. But there is no need for any extended rest if she doesn't want it," the doctor smiles at me.

"See? I'm all good," I say, jumping off the table, wanting out of here before Enzo reads something on my chart or gets some clue that I'm pregnant.

Enzo takes my hands and starts walking me out.

"Oh wait, I have some pain killers for you to take if you need them," the doctor says.

I frown. We never discussed any pain killers. And I doubt pain killers are good for the baby. The only thing we discussed me taking was a prenatal vitamin.

She hands me a container of pills and winks at me. And I suspect these might be prenatal vitamins instead of pain killers.

"Thanks," I say.

Enzo nods, and we walk out of my hospital room, hand in hand.

"You are really okay? Please don't lie to me. I need to know you are okay. Let me take care of you."

I stroke his cheek. "I'm fine. I promise."

He exhales, but I'm not sure if I convinced him or not.

As we walk down the hallway, Enzo catches me up on the status of our team. We didn't lose as many men as I expected after the double explosion. But at least the attack did one thing: get everyone on our side instead of Felix's.

Enzo notices one of our men walking toward us. I don't recall his name, just that he's dressed in dark jeans and black T-shirt, the unofficial uniform of working for us. Enzo drops my hand as soon as he sees him.

I hate that he dropped my hand, even if it's a good idea not to show public displays of affection around the team. Some part of me wants him to say, fuck all of them, and hold my hand like he wants to.

"How many men would be available to attack Felix tomorrow, Carter?" Enzo asks.

"Twenty, possibly more," the man answers.

Enzo gives me a pointed gaze. I'm still in charge. Enzo doesn't get to make this decision. I do.

"Do you think we should attack Felix tomorrow? Give him a little payback for what he did to us?" Enzo asks.

My eyes dart between the two men. I don't want to risk any more lives. I don't want to risk Enzo's life. Or my life. Or our child's life. I've decided this baby has to be Enzo's. *Think positively for once.*

But we need to handle Felix sooner rather than later. Each day that passes, he becomes more dangerous.

"Yes, tomorrow. Tell everyone to meet Enzo and me in the closest bar we own in an hour," I say.

Carter nods and then leaves us.

"The three of us need to have a talk before we meet with the men," I say.

"The three of us?"

"You, me, and Langston."

Enzo tenses, and then takes my hand again as he starts leading me down another hallway.

"No, don't tell me..." If he tells me Langston is dead, I'm going to die. I can't survive another person I love dying.

Enzo grabs my cheeks as the tears burn. "Oh, baby. No, Langston is fine, he's just not in any condition to fight tomorrow."

I sob in relief.

Enzo pulls me into a tight hug, trying to quell my outburst of tears. Langston is fine; I shouldn't be crying. *Maybe it's the pregnancy hormones?* I don't know; I just need to cry.

"Come on, let me show you to his room. It might make you feel better," Enzo says.

We start walking to Langston's room. We peak our head inside and find Liesel laying with her head on one side of Langston's bed.

I raise a knowing eyebrow at the sight of her sleeping next to Langston.

He frowns, shaking his head. "Nothing is going on," he mouths to me.

I grin. Maybe neither of them realize anything is happening between the two of them yet, but they are aloof. Because there is definitely something happening.

I let go of Enzo's hand, who stands near the door to give Langston and me a moment alone.

"How are you feeling?" I ask him, sitting on the other side of the bed across from a sleeping Liesel.

"Better than I look."

I smile weakly. "You do look pretty beat up."

He takes my hand, and his eyes meet mine before dropping to my stomach for the smallest of seconds. Asking me what he needs to without actually saying the words.

I smile the brightest I have in a while thinking about the

memory of hearing my baby's heartbeat for the first time and nod.

He squeezes my hand tighter. "I'm so happy you are going to be alright."

"We need to go. We have to discuss a plan to take out Felix."

He frowns, looking from me to Enzo. "You planning an attack without me?"

"Don't worry, we plan on capturing him and torturing him slowly. So you'll get your shot at him," Enzo says.

"Good," Langston answers.

Liesel snores, and we all giggle at the sudden sound.

"Take care of her," I say, with a wink before kissing Langston's cheek. And then Enzo and I head out of the hospital to the nearest bar we own to discuss how to take out our latest enemy.

———

THE PLAN IS SIMPLE. Felix is staying in a hotel he and his team have taken over. We hacked the hotel's security and found out which room he's staying in. So we will ambush him.

And when I say we, I mean Enzo will lead a team of twenty men, while I will sit watching a security monitor and barking out anything helpful.

If the team doesn't vote Enzo the leader after this, they are crazy. I'm not putting my life at risk to help them, Enzo is.

"You ready?" Enzo asks me from the door of the van I'm hiding in with Arthur and Kent, two of the nerdiest people I've ever met. But if we need to hack any more systems, they are the best we have.

"I should be asking if you are ready. I'm not the one doing anything."

He grins and then kisses me firmly on the lips, not caring who sees us. "You are leading from exactly where you need to be. Just because you don't have skill in hand to hand combat doesn't mean you aren't worthy of leading."

"Go get Felix. He better hope you kill him, because I plan on cutting off his balls for what he's put us through," I say.

"I'll relay the message."

"Good."

His lips hit mine again, and this time, it's not chaste. It's hard and fast. His tongue sweeps into my mouth as he tastes all that he can get of me. I moan back. Only the men staying with me in the van get a view of our makeout session, and I really don't care what they think. Every time Enzo leaves me to go fight a dangerous man could be the last time I get to kiss him, so I make it the best damn kiss I can.

Enzo finally pulls away with a wink.

And then he's gone.

And I'm staring at a grainy computer image, watching as Enzo and team of men and women I'm responsible for sneak into a hotel room to take out Felix.

"Are you okay, Ms. Black?" Arthur asks.

"Uh-huh," I say, my knee bouncing up and down.

He smiles at me. "Mr. Black is the best I've ever seen. A bullet doesn't hit him unless he wants the bullet to hit him. He will take out Felix no problem."

"Thanks, Arthur." But his words don't make me feel any better.

I watch the screen as they break into Felix's room. There is a gunfight, leaving many men injured, but in the end, the fight is between Felix and Enzo. Brother and brother.

They both put their guns down, deciding to fight with just their hands. That should make me feel better. Guns are dangerous, there is only so much damage that can happen when you can only use your fists. But I get a sinking feeling in my belly.

Because as the fight starts, I realize Felix is just as talented a fighter as Enzo. Every other fight I've watched Enzo fight, I know he's going to win. But against Felix, I'm not sure. Their movements are too similar. Their creativity with throwing punches and kicks are on the same level. And the blood they spill from the other is the same.

I cringe with each punch.

But that isn't what has me worried. When I glance at Arthur and Kent, they are just as captivated with what is happening on the screen. They have never seen someone attack Enzo like this. They are in awe of Felix. And if Felix wins, they could decide to make him the new leader.

Fuck, why did we think fighting him was a good idea?

I have to stop this.

I don't think; I just dart out of the van.

"Ms. Black! Wait!" Arthur shouts.

But nothing can stop me. I need to get to Enzo. I need to stop this.

I run through the hotel lobby, choosing the stairs over the elevator even though Felix's room is on the top floor. Floor eleven. My feet can run faster than the elevator can take me.

I reach the floor, panting and sweaty, but I'm relentless. I have the uncontrollable desire to keep going no matter what. I run to the door of the hotel room, throw it open, and the fight stops mid-punch as both men stare at me.

Enzo with fear.

Felix with joy. He thinks this is the moment he wins. He

thinks he'll be able to convince our entire team he deserves to be the leader. I know the men are in awe of his skills, but that's not enough to become Black. It takes a lot more than the ability to fight. It takes bravery and courage and honor —something Felix doesn't have.

"You're fighting the wrong man, don't you think?" I say.

Felix smirks.

Enzo's eyes widen in terror. "Kai, no!"

But Felix grabs Enzo by the neck and tosses him hard to the ground. Enzo was distracted, and Felix didn't fight fair.

"And who should I be fighting? You?" he asks.

"Yes, I'm the leader. I'm Black, not Enzo. Fight me."

Felix's mouth thins, his gaze burns like fire, and his jaw sets in stone. He's trying to understand why I would start a fight I have no chance of winning.

I'm trying to figure it out myself. But the man who is beat up and bloody, still unconscious from Felix's blow is the only answer I can come up with.

Enzo may have been the kind of man who put his own life on the line to fight to protect his men, but I'm counting on my men helping me out with this one. The only way we take Felix is together.

I walk into the center of the room, trying not to worry about Enzo still passed out. Enzo got some good punches in on Felix, his face is covered in blood and cuts, but it wasn't enough. Felix is larger, faster, stronger.

Felix circles me, trying to decide the best way to fight me and still come out looking good to the team.

Come on, Felix. Punch me. In the face, preferably. One punch, and my men will attack.

At least, I hope they will. I've made a good impression on them, but will they risk their lives for me without me giving the order for them to?

I'm about to find out.

"This was foolish of you. You aren't even going to get a punch in before I kill you," Felix says.

"Stop stalling and fight me," I say, putting my fists up.

Felix laughs, stepping closer.

I throw a punch, hitting him as hard as I can in the jaw. *Fuck that hurt my hand.*

And then I see his fist coming down, landing hard against my cheek.

I'm falling. One punch, and I'm going down.

But the men are charging full force against Felix. My last glance before everything goes black isn't of Felix, it's of Enzo stirring in the corner.

I saved his life. I smile, he's safe.

But then I feel an ache in my stomach, and I panic. My baby. *Please, no!* Please don't let me trade one life for another.

19

ENZO

Kai's eyes open.

"Thank God," I say, squeezing her hand in relief as she lies in the bed of one our yachts.

"What happened?" she asks, looking around the room.

"You decided to exchange your life for mine," I give her a stern look.

Her eyes flutter a moment as she tries to remember.

"I was fighting Felix, and then you decided to come in and try to save the day."

She nods. "You were going to lose."

"Then let me lose."

She frowns. "I couldn't watch you die. I had to do something."

"Well, that thing was stupid. You don't get to risk your life to save mine," I growl and grab her shoulders harder than I should, but I need her to realize her life is more valuable than mine. She deserves to live.

She bites her lip. "I know, but don't make me choose again."

"The choice is easy. You choose yourself. Do you under-stand me?"

She nods. "I'm sorry." A tear drips down her cheek.

I brush it off with my thumb, softening.

"Is Felix…"

"We have him. He's locked up in one of the rooms. If you have any doubt whether or not the men respect you more than me, you shouldn't. One punch and they all attacked with a vengeance I haven't seen before."

She nods sadly.

I tilt her chin up so I can look in her eyes. "But then that was your plan the entire time? You knew you couldn't beat Felix yourself."

She nods. "I knew they would fight for me. They wouldn't for you, but only because they are used to you winning by yourself. Protecting them."

"Felix is stronger."

Her eyes narrow, and her hand brushes against my cheek. "Probably, but your heart is bigger. And in the end, that will make the difference."

"I need to kiss you," I plead.

"So kiss me."

I lick my lips and press them against hers, carefully. She took a hard punch to the head. She has a concussion. I need to be gentle with her, even though what I really want to do is throw her over my lap and spank her for thinking she should put herself at risk like that.

Kai kisses me back just as gently. She's equally afraid she's going to break me.

But then she moans, so softly. It's angelic, that moan.

Our eyes both open, staring at each other.

And then all common sense leaves us both.

My lips attack hers, and her hands grip my neck, squeezing so hard it's difficult to breathe. My tongue pushes deep in her mouth, brushing over her glorious tongue. Her nails claw down my neck, not able to get me close enough to her.

"I should be punishing you, not kissing you," I say as I bite her bottom lip.

Her eyes sear. "Then punish me."

The invitation to punish her does things to my cock I'm not proud of. I shouldn't enjoy hurting her in any way. But I get hard all the same.

I have to be careful with her. I don't want to hurt her. But I want her to know how serious I am about her not risking her life again for mine. And I need to taste her. A plan forms in my head as I kiss down her body.

"What are you doing?" she asks as I kiss over her stomach before pulling down the boxer shorts she's wearing.

My eyes widen at the beautiful sight.

"Punishing you," I say as my lips go straight for her clit. Sucking and nipping, pleasuring her too much at once.

She arches her back at the surge of deliciousness pulsing through her body.

"How is this punishing me?" she moans.

I flick my tongue over her clit again. "Because I'm not going to let you come."

"What?" she throws her head up in a panic and tries to push my head off her, but I just grip her legs tighter and bury my head between her legs.

"Enzo, stop! If you aren't going to let me come then..." her arguing stops though as I slide one finger through her slickness.

I pump her once, twice, feeling her spread open for me. I pull my finger all the way out and slip another in as I continue to torture her clit with my tongue.

I feel her getting close. I feel her body tightening around my fingers.

And then I stop.

"You bastard. Make me come!" Kai cries.

"Not until you've learned your lesson. You don't trade your life for mine. Never again. I thought you would learn your lesson with Milo. He took everything from us when you traded your life for mine."

She stares angrily at me.

"I didn't have a choice! I couldn't watch you die."

"And I can't watch you die either."

My thumb circles her clit again, bringing her close before denying her.

"Say it."

She glares.

"Say you won't ever trade your life for mine again. That you will never come to my rescue again."

"Only if you promise to never put yourself at risk unnecessarily again."

"I promise," I say.

She swallows hard as I press my thumb against her button, but I don't move. I just hold it there, waiting.

"I promise," she says, with sincerity in her eyes.

It's the best I'm going to get for now.

So I stop torturing both of us. I push my finger inside of her, and one flick of my tongue sends her into a spiraling orgasm.

So beautiful.

When she's come down from her high, I pull my fingers

out of her and lick them, before licking my way up her body, examining every inch of her as I go. I had the doctor look her over, and all he determined was that she had a concussion and needed some rest, but I need to survey every inch of her to be sure.

I kiss over her legs, not noticing any new bruises or cuts. I've already examined her perfect pussy. And then I kiss over her stomach. It's swollen, but I don't notice any bruising yet. *Is something happening internally?*

"What's wrong?" she asks, stroking my hair.

"Nothing, does anything hurt?"

"No," she stretches.

I don't want to worry her about internal bleeding. I'll have the doctor take a look again.

I keep kissing up her body when a knock on the door interrupts me.

I sigh and get off her as she slides her shorts back up.

"Yes?" I say grumpily.

The door opens, and Archard and the five voting members stand at the door before filing into the room.

"What's going on?" Kai asks.

"The month is up. It's time for the final vote," Archard says.

Kai noticeably tenses. I take her hand. There is no reason to hide my feelings from the team. They know how I feel.

"Alright, then let's start the vote. You are not voting for who is doing the best at this very moment, but who you think won the game overall and who you'd rather see as your leader moving forward," Archard says.

Clifton starts, "Enzo."

I raise an eyebrow.

And Kai smiles. She'd rather have me win.

I'm torn. I want to win. I want her to win. But most of all, I want more time with her. I want her safe. And I don't know which way results in getting everything I want.

Odette goes next, "Kai."

"Kai."

"Kai."

"Kai."

Kai wins.

I've never been prouder and more terrified in my life.

"Thank you for assisting with this round. I need to speak to Kai and Enzo alone," Archard says.

A few moments later, we are alone with Archard.

"You are now tied, two to two," he says.

Kai and I both nod.

"Which means you will both participate in the final round."

We both suck in a breath as Archard speaks, like his words will decide the fate of our entire future.

No, fuck him. We will decide our own futures, not anyone else.

"When will the game happen?" I ask.

"Well, as far as I'm aware, neither of you have finalized your heirs." Archard looks to me. "You originally put down Milo's child as your heir, but as he died before having a child, I will need you to select again."

Archard looks at Kai. "And as you haven't been able to find any family ties left, you will need to have a child of your own to have an heir."

Kai flinches as Archard says she will need to get pregnant. *She can't, you asshole.* But I don't speak the words out loud because I don't want to hurt Kai.

"You both have one year to figure out your heir."

"And what if neither of us can find an heir?" I ask.

"Then it will go to a team vote. The men and women who work for you can decide if they will allow you to select heirs not blood-related, or if they would like to select new competitors outside of either of your families to compete in the games to become their leaders."

"Why do we need blood heirs?" Kai asks.

"I can't answer that yet. Your questions will be answered at the final game."

Kai looks like she wants to kill Archard. I agree, but don't act. As soon as the final game is over, I plan on killing him.

Archard starts walking toward the door. "I've explained everything for now. For the next year, or until you have both named heirs, you will continue to make decisions about the organization together. And remember you both have to produce separate heirs."

And then we are alone again.

"Well, I guess that decides it. Felix will rule," I say, kissing her neck again.

She tenses. "Why do you say that?"

"Because the only child I plan on having is with you. And since the only way we will have a child together is adoption, and therefore won't be blood related to either of us, we will have to give the company up."

"You can't do that. This is your life."

"No, you're my life." I kiss her hard on the lips, planning on showing her just how much my words are true.

"Enzo, I need to tell you something."

I sit back, waiting for her to talk.

But before she can speak, there is another knock at the door.

"I hope you are both decent because Langston and I are coming in," Liesel says.

Kai's face goes pale, but she quickly shakes it off.

"We will talk later," I say, kissing her lips.

But from the worried look on her face, whatever she was planning on talking to me about is important.

20

KAI

I'm GOING to tell Enzo about the baby. He needs to know. It's the only way to make the right decision. All I know is my child can't be the heir. I won't let any child of mine go through this pain.

But Enzo needs to find an heir. We can't let Felix have this kind of power.

I open my mouth several times to tell Enzo I'm pregnant as Liesel, Langston, Enzo, and I talk. But it doesn't seem like the right moment, to tell him that he's going to be a father in front of them. Or he's going to be an uncle. I don't know which one, but I prefer to think of Enzo as the father. At least that's how I plan on breaking the news to him.

But I can't in front of Liesel and Langston. Especially since they both know. It would hurt Enzo to know they knew before him.

Liesel carries most of the conversation, talking about random company gossip instead of the seriousness of what is happening. Every once in a while, I see Langston and Liesel sneak a secret look at each other, and it's almost as if they are staying to keep me from talking to Enzo. But that can't be true. I'd think they would both want me to tell him.

"We need to interrogate Felix and then kill him. We can't trust him. He's smart and sneaky. He may have even planned on getting captured. He's fearless and unpredictable. We need to get all the answers we can get from him and get rid of him before he does more damage," Enzo says.

We all nod in agreement.

"Langston come with me. Liesel, keep Kai company until we get back," Enzo says.

"Hell no!" Liesel and I both say at the same time.

Both men turn, frowning at us.

"We are coming," Liesel says, with her hands on her hips.

I nod. "Yes, we are coming. Every time we are separated, something bad happens. We are all part of this. Felix is tied up; he can't hurt us. We all need answers."

"You are not coming. You have a concussion. You are staying in bed," Enzo says.

"I'm coming," I say, getting out of bed. I grab a pair of jeans draped over a chair in the corner and put them on.

Enzo frowns.

So does Langston.

But I'm not taking no for an answer.

And neither is Liesel.

"Remember what you promised?" Enzo asks me.

I nod. "Remember what you promised me?" I hiss.

He nods solemnly.

"Good, then neither of us will put our lives at risk. We are just going to talk," I say.

"And kill that son of a bitch," Liesel says, but I'm not sure if she's trying to lighten the mood or be serious.

Langston sighs. "Let's get this over with."

We all walk to the room trapping Felix. Langston in front, followed by Liesel, with Enzo and me holding hands taking up the rear.

That's how we all march into Felix's room.

I shut the door hard behind me. No one else will get to talk to him. This is personal.

Felix is lying on a bed with his hands chained above his head, and his feet tied together.

"Are we about to do some kinky shit?" Felix asks, winking at me.

"No, we are about to torture and kill you," I say, my eyes sinking into his.

"Sounds like a kinky party to me," he responds.

We all glare or growl at him, which only makes him chuckle harder.

"Fine, let's do this the easy way. What do you want to know?" he asks.

I widen my eyes and look at Enzo. *Why is he making this easy?*

Enzo steps forward, so I do too. We are a united front. He moves, I move.

"We want access to the weapons you have. The security systems you employ. We want the name of every person who works for you. We want to know any booby traps you have planned. Any explosions that haven't been set off," Enzo says.

Felix rolls his eyes. "Of course, you are asking the wrong questions. But get me a pen and paper, and I'll write every password, code, and weapon down. I won't give you names of my men though. I'm not a snitch like you."

"What is that supposed to mean?" Enzo asks.

"Unlike you, I'm loyal to my men."

Enzo growls. "I'm loyal to my men."

Felix purses his lips. "If I told you there are bombs set to go off on every ship you own, killing all your men instantly, but I would give you the information to stop the detonations in exchange for Kai, what would you say?"

"Fuck you," Enzo says.

I rub Enzo's arm, trying to calm him down. Felix is just goading us.

"Which would you choose? The whore or your men?"

"Both, and then I'd kill you for threatening them."

He shakes his head. "And if I were about to rape your woman?"

Felix pushed too far. Enzo is across the bed, punching Felix in the face over and over. Blood squirts everywhere.

And the three of us watch, not stopping Enzo. Felix deserves to die for what he's done.

Finally, Enzo stops. "Don't threaten Kai."

"Just Kai? I thought this was about your men."

Enzo steps back, happy with the damage he's done to Felix's face.

"I love Kai; I won't deny it. There is no reason to. Not anymore. You lost. You will never walk out of this room again. You will die here on this bed."

I intertwine my fingers with Enzo's. "And I love him. You did your best to break us up. You tried to turn our own team against us, but you lost. We win. Love wins."

"Look at the two of you, so happy and in love. You are in love with the prince. And he's in love with his princess. Except neither of you is worthy of the title."

Felix looks at Enzo. "You killed your own brother in cold blood. He did nothing wrong, and you killed him."

He looks at me. *No, he looks at my stomach.* "And you are

hiding a secret. I know it. And soon your men will know it. You are supposed to be loyal to them and them alone."

Felix knows I'm pregnant, I can see it in his snake eyes. He knows. *How did he figure it out before Enzo did?* My stomach did pop overnight. There is a small bump beneath the baggy shirt I'm wearing, but it's not enough to confirm it. And I'm not discussing it with Felix.

"Kill him, Enzo. He's done telling us anything important," I say.

I look at Langston and Liesel, who are standing defiant behind us. Langston has his gun drawn like he wants to be the one to kill Felix.

But Enzo draws his weapon too.

Felix grins.

Something feels wrong, but what?

I squeeze Enzo's hand, silently warning him.

He shoots me a glance, and I know he gets the message. We should have just killed Felix without talking to him. But we are all ready for whatever Felix is trying to pull.

Suddenly, our phones all buzz at the same time.

Enzo, Langston, and I ignore it, but Liesel answers.

"What the hell did you do?" her words are directed to Felix.

Felix snickers. "I told everyone the truth."

Liesel walks up to Enzo and me, holding her phone out to us.

Our mouths fall open as we look at the video. It's of us, planting a bomb on our ship. *How did Felix doctor this? How did he do this?*

"That is being sent out to every member of your team."

"Why would they believe that we would blow up our ship? Our own men?" I ask.

"So you could play rescuer. So they would think you were trying to protect them."

Fuck.

Felix laughs.

He just won.

I glance at the cameras zooming in on us. The security cameras have been watching us this whole time. The men and women who work for us were watching. They heard our declarations of love for each other. They see the video evidence that we aren't on their side.

"Enzo," I say softly, because I feel the danger approaching.

His eyes read mine one second before the danger hits.

The door bursts open as Enzo and Langston fire their gun. I run to the window, popping it open as Felix did before.

"If I had a gun, I'd kill you," I say to Felix.

"Then I guess you'll owe me," he says with a wink.

And then I'm pulling Liesel out the window, hoping the guys follow, but not before they shoot Felix in the head.

21

ENZO

WHAT IS STOPPING me from killing this bastard? I should have killed Felix the second I stepped foot into this room. Instead, I tried to get answers.

What is wrong with me?

Why can't I kill him?

Is it because he's my brother? Because we share blood? What?

Kai and Liesel went out the window while Langston and I get shot at by men who swore an oath to this organization. Men who have fought alongside me. Put their lives in my hands are now fighting me. Trying to kill me.

"Go," I shout to Langston.

He dives out the window while I hold off the men long enough to lock the door.

"You can't kill me. I'm the only one with answers," Felix says.

I don't give a fuck about his answers, because I no longer have any questions.

I dive out the window, firing one last shot at Felix's head.

I miss.

I never fucking miss.

Something is off with me, and I don't know what it is. But I need to get it fixed fast, or we are all going to die because I can't protect those I love.

Kai, Liesel, and Langston are climbing into a dingy boat while half my team shoots at us and the other half stand frozen, unsure of how to react.

I jump in the boat, and Kai hits the gas, while Langston and I provide cover fire while we make our escape.

Finally, we are far enough away that the bullets can no longer hit us.

I slump into the chair, not believing what is happening. My own men firing at me.

"Not everyone turned on you. There were men and women who didn't shoot. There are some still loyal to you," Langston says, like his words should comfort me.

"And there are plenty who are no longer loyal. Plenty who would rather follow an evil bastard like Felix than me," I say.

Langston nods. "Yes, but you already knew that. The men who will follow Felix are the same who blindly followed your father. They like torturing people for no reason. They like killing. They like buying and selling people like property. That is what your father did for extra cash before you came along."

"I'm no better," I say.

"Yes, you are," all three say in unison.

I sigh, staring out at the ocean. We aren't safe here; we need a plan. We need to head somewhere secure.

"Drive us home," I tell Langston.

He frowns. "Your house isn't safe."

"It's safe enough. We have protection there. Security only I know about. It will give us enough time to form a plan," I say. *Although, I already know the plan.* Get Liesel and Kai somewhere safe. Contact any of the men we think are still on our side. And then kill Felix and any of his followers.

Langston trades places with Kai and starts driving us toward my house on the beach. If they kill me, I'd rather die in my own home.

And if we succeed in killing Felix, the team won't have a choice but to choose Kai or me as the leader when the time comes. Even if neither of us has an heir.

"I need to talk to you."

I expect the words to be coming from Kai, but it's Liesel who is speaking.

"Okay," I say with a deep frown. "Now, or do you want to talk in private?"

I notice Langston tense, and Kai's eyes drop to her lap like there is something very interesting she needs to pay attention to on her thigh.

"No, we need to talk now. And everyone can hear," she says.

I nod for her to begin, not having a clue what is so important that needs to be said right now.

"I know you are both worried about having an heir. Even if you kill Felix, the only way to ensure one of his followers doesn't gain power and ruin hundreds of innocent lives is to have an heir. If you have an heir and win the final game, then that's it. No one can question your authority," she says.

"Yes, I guess that's true," I say, but I do not like where this is going. No one on the boat does.

Langston's face is turning angrier by the second. I can see a vein popping out of his head, and his nostrils flaring.

And Kai keeps trying to sink into her chair until she vanishes.

Kai is the only one I want a child with, and she can't have children. And even if she could, I'm not sure our joint child would be accepted. Not after half of our team shot at us.

But if Liesel is suggesting her and I have a child together, everyone on this boat is going to lose it.

I try to be patient, to wait for her to speak, but my anger gets the best of me.

"Liesel, you can't be seriously suggesting that I fuck you to get you pregnant?" I half say, half yell.

The boat lurches to the side as Langston takes a turn too sharp. We all grab on, emotions flowing too much.

Liesel looks like she's about to cry.

"Just listen to her, Enzo. That's not what she's trying to tell you," Kai says, taking Liesel's hand in hers and squeezing it.

Langston doesn't speak, but it's clear he isn't happy.

And I don't understand what is happening at all.

"I have a child," Liesel says.

I narrow my eyes, not understanding.

"What? No, you don't. I would have known about it. We've never gone nine months without seeing each other," I say.

"I hid it. I didn't get big until close to the end, and at that point, you were pretty busy with other things," Liesel says.

Liesel has a child? That's crazy. But incredible. Liesel would make a great mom. Except, I've never seen her with a child.

"I gave him up after he was born. I didn't want him anywhere near this life."

I nod, it makes sense. If given the choice, I wouldn't want any child of mine in this world.

The boat has stopped, and Langston's eyes are wide on Liesel. *He didn't know.*

But Kai is still holding Liesel's hand, nodding for her to go on. *Kai knew.* This was the secret Liesel shared to gain Kai's trust. And the more I see how Kai is looking at Liesel, the more afraid I am.

"How old is your son?"

Liesel's eyes are heavy. "Three-years-old."

Fuck.

The child's mine.

How could she have not told me? How could I have not have been part of his life? Or at least allowed to hold him before she gave him up?

Kai backs away, wanting to give us a moment.

But Liesel speaks up. "The child isn't yours."

"What? How?"

"Because he's your brother."

My heart stops. I've had it up to here with finding out I have half-brothers.

"What?"

She swallows hard.

"Your father. He...again."

My father raped her again. I couldn't save her. I can never save the ones I love.

Tears drip down my face.

All I can focus on is the drip.

Drip.

Drip.

Drip.

I'm numb.

I don't move.

I've let so many people I love get hurt. I've never been strong enough to stop it from happening. *Never.* It never stops hurting, finding out I failed.

I can't even apologize for not stopping him. *How did I*

miss this? How did I not realize he raped her again? It had to have happened right before I killed him. Why didn't I kill him sooner?

Liesel starts talking again, so I do my best to listen. "I don't want to talk about how it happened. But I didn't want you to feel guilty. And I also didn't want you to have anything to do with the child. Not because you wouldn't have made a great stand-in father, but because having the child was my choice. And putting him up for adoption was my choice as well."

"Why are you telling me now?"

"You deserve to know you have a three-year-old half-brother somewhere. You have an heir if you need him to be. All I ask is that you do everything in your power to protect him if he ends up in this world."

Liesel's on the verge of tears. So I do what I should have done from the beginning—I pull her into a hug.

"Shh, he's safe. He doesn't belong here. You did the right thing by giving him up, Liesel. The brave, strong thing. I'm so proud of you," I say into her hair, as I grip her as tight as I can, trying to take her pain.

"No, put his name down on the contract. You deserve to have control of the Black empire. There is no one better to ensure the technology, the security systems, the bombs, the weapons, the money doesn't fall into the wrong hands. There is no man I know who would ensure the right thing is done, not just the thing to make the most money. You care about the people who work for you. You care about the people who hire you for security. You care about the women who have been stolen by other criminal organizations you do business with. Put his name down on the damn paper. Win your empire, and then change the damn rules before he turns eighteen," Liesel says.

I give her a tight smile. I can't promise her I will or won't use his name. I don't like bringing an innocent child into this world, but if it's my only choice, I will.

"Thank you for telling me, Liesel," I say.

She nods. "I couldn't keep the secret anymore. You deserve to know. And I trust you with his life."

22

———

KAI

Liesel is either the strongest woman I know, or she's a bitch who is trying to steal my man and make me feel bad for keeping my secret while spilling her own.

But when she looks at me with tears in her eyes, I know she's on my side.

All she did was open the door for me. Give me insight into how Enzo my react to me telling him I'm pregnant. He would protect the child. No matter if the child is his or my rapist's. No matter if this child is the only way to get power, he won't use my child that way unless I beg him to. And even then, he probably wouldn't.

I can trust him with my secret.

But as soon as I speak the words, my secret is out there. It's like when I loved him but couldn't say it. The truth spoken is one that can never be taken back.

And I'm scared.

Not that Enzo wouldn't hide my secret from the world. Not that this baby wouldn't be safe with him protecting him or her. But scared that by admitting I'm pregnant out loud, I will be saying I have to leave Enzo.

Enzo doesn't just deserve to be the leader of Black. Liesel is right; the world needs him to be. Before Enzo, the Black organization was just a group of thieves in the night. They stole from the rich and the poor. They sold drugs. They sold people. They sold weapons to the highest bidder, not caring if that bidder was evil and would use them to kill people. They dabbled in everything and killed everyone and everything that opposed them. But since Enzo has taken over, he has steered them into a more honorable way of getting money. They aren't saints, but the evil they do doesn't destroy innocent lives.

They only take from their enemies. They only steal from those who deserve to be stolen from. They don't sell people. And they only sell weapons to those who won't turn around and try to take out entire countries.

Enzo has to stay in this world.

And I have to leave—for my child's sake.

I feel my eyes watering, but I have to be strong, like Liesel. Except Liesel gets to stay. I can't give my child up for adoption. My child would be far more valuable than Liesel's. Because if an enemy kidnapped my child, they could get Enzo to do anything to get that child back.

"Enzo..." I start, then stop.

I'm not sure I should have this conversation in front of Langston and Liesel, but they both know my secret. Liesel gets up and walks over to Langston, giving me a quick nod that it's time. Langston gives me a tight smile, and I know he approves as well. It's now or never.

My eyes flutter to meet Enzo's heavy gaze. I should be sitting right next to him, holding his hand as I deliver my news. But I can't. I'm frozen. Too scared to lose him.

I don't know how to live without Enzo Black.

But if I keep him, he will no longer be Enzo Black. He

will return to being Enzo Rinaldi. A man who never existed. He wouldn't be the man I fell in love with. He has to stay Enzo Black.

We gaze into each other's eyes. Frozen in time. Enzo's eyes still carry tears from hearing he has a younger brother. I still wasn't sure until Liesel spoke that her child wasn't also Enzo's. And I'm grateful her child isn't, even though that's selfish of me. Even though having a child caused her pain. My eyes are filling with my own lonely tears. But I will not cry when I tell him my news. So I suck the tears in and let my lips fall into something like a smile.

"Enzo, I—"

He presses a finger to my lips, stopping me from speaking.

His eyes change to a darker shade of brown as he looks over my body, taking in all the clues he missed before: my swollen breasts, my growing belly, my morning sickness.

Our worlds stop, and we have the most private moment we've ever had. It doesn't matter that Langston and Liesel are there, because we don't need words.

You're pregnant, his eyes say.

Yes.

A tiny smile.

Bright eyes.

He's happy, overjoyed even.

I smile back at him, letting myself glow for the first time since I found out I was pregnant.

Enzo takes my hand, and I let him.

In this moment, we are happy, expecting parents sharing a secret only the two of us know. It doesn't matter that in reality, Langston and Liesel know. Or that Felix knows. All that matters is our little secret happiness.

I love you, he mouths.

I love you too, I mouth back.

I feel the wind blowing in my face again as Langston starts driving the boat again. But it doesn't shake our little moment. This single moment is the happiest I've ever been. And it appears Enzo feels the same.

This is happiness.

This is love.

He doesn't ask me any questions.

Not if it's his or Milo's.

Not how far along I am.

Not if I know if it's a boy or girl.

Not what are we going to do.

The questions don't matter. What matters is that no matter the answers, we are both desperately in love with this child.

We ride in silence holding each other's hands and gazing into each other's eyes until we reach Enzo's house.

Langston goes in first, wanting a moment to secure the property before the rest of us enter.

When he gives us the all-clear, we enter. Langston and Liesel retreat to separate guest bedrooms, and Enzo carries me up the stairs to the bedroom we've shared so many memories together in.

"Enzo, we need to talk," I say.

"No, I don't want to talk about this until we can only speak happy, excited words. I won't tarnish something so happy with fear and anxiety. We don't need to speak—not today. And we don't need to worry about what this means or what tomorrow holds. Just be with me tonight, Kai. Love me. Remind me of how incredible we are together. And how nothing can stop us as long as we love each other. That's all I want."

"Okay," I whisper, because I can barely breathe.

And that is the last word I will speak tonight. Because if either of us starts talking, we won't be able to focus on just loving each other. The topic will change to worry and how to protect this child. And tonight, we both just need each other.

I grab the hem of my shirt and pull it over my head, letting my body be on full display for him.

His eyes grow at the sight. I can tell he's a little frustrated with himself for not realizing sooner.

He lifts his own shirt, and I ogle his firm body that has saved me more times than he realizes.

My hand goes to my hair, and I pull my scrunchie out and put it on my wrist, my hair falling down in waves.

Enzo's eyes deepen at the sight.

Simultaneously, we remove our pants, naked in front of each other.

Vulnerable, scared, and happy.

Enzo is taking his time gazing at me, trying to study every curve, because the second he touches me we won't be able to stop and slow down. But his gaze is driving me crazy.

I whimper under his hungry gaze.

He smirks.

And then we collide.

Our bodies.

Our hearts.

Our love.

His hands grab my ass, and I wrap my legs around his, wishing I had heels on to dig into his back.

Tongues sweep through each other's mouths. Moans purr down each other's throats.

And before I realize what is happening, I'm straddling

him on the bed. His hard cock pressed against my opening, all I have to do is press down, and he'll be inside me.

I like the power I have sitting on top of him, but not entering. Enzo's frown tells me he doesn't like me torturing him at all. But it only seems fair.

Slowly, I slide down onto his cock. And I've never felt more whole. The way he fills me with the hint of a burn, but mostly delicious stretching until I take all of him, is everything.

I rock back and forth as our eyes lock again.

I love you.

I love you, too.

More rocking as pleasure shoots through me, and we continue our silent exchange of words.

I love him, he says, referencing the baby.

What if he's a her?

Then I'll love her, too.

I smile, but soon I won't be able to focus on anything but the intense feeling between my legs.

I'm scared.

I want him to take away my fear. I want him to promise me to protect me like he has before. That no one will ever hurt me. Instead, he says with his body...

Me too.

And then he bucks harder. And I ride him hard and fast. The nerve endings spread the pleasure all over my body.

Until I'm coming, and he's filling me with his orgasm.

I collapse on his body, and he rolls me over as he pulls out. He breaks our vow of silence as he kisses my stomach.

"Mine," he says, kissing my lower belly.

He doesn't say it as a question. As if he's wondering whose child it is, Milo's or his. He doesn't seem to care. He is taking ownership over the child no matter whose it is genetically.

Mine is now my favorite word, I think as I fall asleep in Enzo's arms.

23

ENZO

Kai is pregnant.

With my baby.

Or at least that is what I'm choosing to believe. I don't ever want her to do a DNA test. The baby is mine. *He's mine.* I don't know the sex either, but I'm guessing it's a him. So that's what I call him in my head.

A baby.

My baby.

Kai is pregnant.

How is that possible?

All the doctors said it wasn't possible.

But she just made everything possible.

She's pregnant.

And Liesel had my father's child. He raped her. And she had his child.

Kai could be...

No, don't go there. The baby is mine, not Milo's. Even if it is technically his, it will be hard to tell. Milo was my half-brother. The child will look like me, no matter what.

But I won't get to be there for the child.

The child needs to disappear. No one wants us to have a child together.

They want me and Kai to fight. To hate each other. To prove the strongest to them. Then raise our children to do the same.

We both have heirs.

Kai has her child.

And I could claim Liesel's.

But if we did that, I could never claim Kai's child as mine, and he's mine! I won't ever pretend otherwise.

So it's better off if we hide the child, like Liesel did. Hide our child away.

I have to stay. Become Mr. Black.

Kai will want to go with the child to protect him.

And I won't ever be able to search for them, not if I want to keep them safe. They will have to be hidden, even from me.

What if there is another way?

What if I can keep Kai and my child?

Then I would have to give up the empire.

If the choice is between Kai and my child or the empire, the choice is easy. I will always choose Kai and my son.

But I've never been able to protect them before. I've never been able to protect those I love. They are better off without me.

But maybe that's the problem...

I've never been able to choose before. I always tried to do both. I tried to be Mr. Black, while also protecting those I love. That's why I always failed.

I won't fail this time because I'll give one of them up—the empire.

But I can't let them be ruled by Felix. For one, we would never be safe. He'd chase us to the ends of the earth.

A plan forms in my head as I hold the two most precious people in the world. Kai rests her head on my chest, and I rest my hand over her tiny stomach. I want to take her to get an ultrasound as soon as possible. I want to see my child. But I'll wait until it's safe. Just like I'll wait to have our first conversation about our baby until it's safe.

I hated the conversation with Liesel. It was filled with worry, pain, and sadness. I don't want that for our child. Only happiness and love will surround any conversation about our child.

So I continue to form a plan.

Kill Felix, that is at the top of the list.

Win the game.

Then change the rules, giving someone like Langton or Odette control. Maybe even have another, less gruesome, competition, so the men will believe the person who takes over is worthy.

Only then will Kai, our baby, and I run away. We will disappear. We will be safe. We will live in the woods or on a farm, somewhere where no one will find us. But it won't matter, because all we will need is each other.

24

KAI

I KNOW the moment everything changes.

Our tiny moment of happiness—gone.

Enzo and Langston have spent the last few hours finding every man and woman on our side and getting them to this house. Our quiet sanctuary is now filled with men with guns.

"I still don't understand. Why are so many following Felix? He tried to attack them. He tried to kill them. Can't they see he's evil?" Liesel asks.

"Because they are scared. They see love as a weakness. And some of them prefer a leader like Felix. He told them all he's Enzo's brother. So he's a Rinaldi. They've seen how strong he is in a fight. And they think he will return the organization to the old ways—raping women, selling people, building dangerous weapons to sell to even more dangerous criminals, murdering innocent people," Clifton says.

"Well, they are deranged if they think Felix is a better leader than Enzo or Kai," Liesel says.

Clifton smiles at her. "That's why so many of us are here." He winks at her, giving her his dirtiest smile.

And Langston tenses from across the room. I walk over to him. "Are you ever going to do anything about your feelings?"

"I don't have any feelings," he answers.

I raise an eyebrow.

"I don't."

I shake my head but quickly forget about Langston and Liesel's unrequited love. Because I suddenly feel like I'm being covered by a cloud of doom.

Langston notices my reaction. "Kai, what's happening?"

He assumes something is wrong with the baby. But it's not.

"I think—" I start.

Enzo is by my side immediately. "Felix is here."

I nod, agreeing.

"You saw him on the security cameras? How many men did he bring?" Langston asks.

Enzo shakes his head. "He hasn't shown up yet on the security cameras. It's just a feeling I have."

I take his hand. "Me too."

Liesel spots our little pow wow, and walks over. She reads the fear in all of our eyes. "He's here?"

We all nod.

I tighten my grip on Enzo's hands because I know what the plan is. And I hate the plan.

But I also know, I have no choice.

"Kai?" Liesel says, telling me it's time. I should have left long ago. Before Felix arrived. But I couldn't bring myself to leave Enzo. I have to now.

I have to choose—Enzo or the baby.

I can't protect them both.

Enzo can take care of himself, but it still kills me I can't be here, fighting alongside him. I won't know for hours if he lived or died.

But I don't have a choice. I have to put my baby first.

I grab Enzo's neck pulling him into the deepest kiss I've ever given him.

He kisses me back with everything he has, like he's trying to exchange his heart and soul with mine. And I pour everything back, giving him a part of me to take with him always.

If there was ever a question about how we felt about each other, it's gone now. No one who witnessed the kiss could see it as anything but an exchange of love.

"Kai!" I hear Liesel's voice trying to break through my happy fog. I don't want to go. I want to stay. I need to say.

Go, Enzo mouths.

And then he's pulling away, while I'm gasping for more.

Our fingers are still intertwined, but that is all that is left.

"I love you, stingray."

I hold back my sobs. Be strong. He doesn't need to see you cry moments before he takes on his greatest foe.

"I love you, too," I say, expelling all of my air as I speak. I have nothing left.

His heated eyes stare down to my belly and then back to my eyes, telling me to take care of our baby.

I nod, I will.

Then Liesel takes my other hand, and she's pulling me away.

My eyes go to where Enzo and my's hands still cling to each other. I watch as our hands are slowly pulled apart, until only our fingertips are touching. And then the connection breaks.

Enzo puts his hands in the pockets of his jeans as Liesel continues to pull me away.

I don't pay attention to where we are walking; my gaze is still on his—soaking up every last drop of him.

Until we turn a corner.

And Enzo is gone.

"Come on, babe. You got this. Enzo and Langston are going to be fine," Liesel says.

But she's clearly trying to reassure herself as much as she's trying to reassure me.

I nod, though.

Our plan is simple. Liesel and I are getting as far the hell away from here. We are going to hide somewhere. The boys don't even know where we are going. Liesel and I haven't even discussed a location.

But in two days, we are going to call Enzo's phone from a payphone, and if the threat is over, we will return. And if no one answers, then we will keep running and hiding, forever.

If Enzo and Langston are alive, they will come find us. And if they are dead, then at least Liesel and I will be safe. The baby will be safe.

We both climb into the SUV at the back of the property, an Escalade with bulletproof windows. It would take a tank to stop this car, Enzo said.

Liesel drives.

We are headed to a helicopter Enzo arranged to take us to an airport in Atlanta. From there, we can buy tickets anywhere. We have new identities. And lots of cash. No one will be able to find us unless we want them to.

Please find us soon, Enzo.

Liesel steps on the gas, driving through a back road off the property.

Only then when the house starts getting small in the

rearview mirror do I let the tears fall. But I'm not the only one. Liesel is crying too. Because we are both driving away from the men we love. I'm not sure who Liesel is crying for —Enzo or Langston. I know she loves Enzo. I hope she loves Langston. But it doesn't matter; the heartbreak is the same.

I reach over and grip her hand. We can do this, together.

We both take a deep breath.

It's going to be okay.

But it's never okay.

Danger follows me everywhere I go.

And the explosion ringing in my ears, the smoke billowing all around, and the fire burning as the SUV rolls over and over all remind me I will never be safe.

25

ENZO

I've spent the last few hours debating whether to implant every tracking device imaginable into Kai and Liesel's phones, clothing, car, everything. I need to know where they are. I need to know they are safe.

But I decided against it.

Because if I can't find them, then neither can Felix.

"It's going to be okay," Langston says as soon as Kai and Liesel are gone.

I glare at him. "Don't say that. I hate that saying. You don't know everything is going to be okay."

"I know," he frowns.

"Then, why the fuck did you say it?" I ask as I load my guns and make sure I have plenty of ammo.

He shrugs. "Because this is hard for me, too."

I roll my eyes. "You are just infatuated with Liesel; she will never like you back. Get over it, man."

Langston looks like he's about to kill me. "Why? Because you like her still hung up on you?"

"No, I want her happy. And you aren't the settling down kind."

"Whatever, let's just kill this bastard and everyone else on his side. Then we can argue about whether or not I'd make a good boyfriend," he says.

I hold out my hand, and he grasps it. "Deal."

Before we can move, explosions start erupting.

Fuck, I hate Felix Black.

He can't even fight like a man; he has to resort to using explosives—ones I'm sure my company made.

Langston and I dive down, covering our heads as my home begins to crumble around us.

"The girls…" Langston's voice breaks.

"They got out okay."

He frowns. "Now, who is bullshitting for no reason?"

"We don't have time to argue now." I grab his hand and pull him up after I stand.

And then we break apart, barking orders and pulling up the security feed to see where Felix is.

I spot him, standing smugly at the entrance—waiting for me.

He wants a fight—one on one.

I smile; it's exactly what I want.

He may have won our last fight. But that was before I found out I'm going to be a father.

Kai is away. There will be no distractions.

I no longer care that Felix is my brother. I don't feel guiltly for killing our brother. I want this fight. I want to kill Felix myself.

I walk outside with my gun pointed at Felix. I'm not going to wait for an invitation to fight this time; I start pulling the trigger—aiming at Felix as he dives behind a car.

Several of his men are standing around, expecting to watch a show. But they won't get to spectate. I shoot them all, killing them one by one. *The traitorous bastards.* They all used to work for me. Fight by my side. I protected them endless times fighting battles by myself, only involving them in the fight when I had to, and this is how they repay me.

"Come out and fight," I say, when the smoke clears.

Felix is still hiding behind the car, but I hear his chuckles. *Everything is a joke with this guy.*

I hear the bullets flying before I see them, and I dive down as I fire back.

We continue to exchange bullets. For hours. Both of us ducking behind bulletproof cars as we try to fire at the other. And I know eventually, we will run out of bullets.

I could text Langston to meet me with more bullets, but he's busy fighting off the rest of Felix's team.

No, I want to kill Felix by myself.

I look at the dozen bullets I have left. I can't keep shooting at a car. I need to attack.

I move silently, ducking behind cars, making it impossible for Felix to know where I am. He doesn't know which side I'm attacking from or how close I am, but since I'm no longer firing bullets at him, he knows I'm close. He knows I'm about to attack.

I pull a knife from my pocket, ready for hand to hand combat.

And then I jump over the car Felix is hiding behind. Father may have taught him many things, but he's not as skilled as I am at hiding or moving silently. Felix's heavy breathing told me exactly where he was at all times.

I get one good slice in before he attacks back. I knock the gun from his hand as I punch him in the face.

Fighting isn't supposed to be personal. You aren't supposed to let any emotions in. That's what father used to say. The winner only wins because he can separate his emotions from the fight.

I disagree.

Each punch is personal.

It's retaliation for threatening Kai's life.

For threatening to take our love away.

For threatening my son's life.

And the more I let my emotions in, the harder I fight.

I'm winning.

I know it.

Felix knows it.

And there are none of his men here to save him. Not this time. *This time I win.*

But the thing about fighting in real life, unlike the boxing ring, it doesn't matter if you've been winning the entire time. You don't get points for throwing better punches. You don't win because you are the better fighter. In real life, one punch is all it takes. One slice of the blade. One shot of the gun.

But none of those is Felix's style. No, he prefers to attack with his brain rather than his fists. And he knows exactly where to get me—my heart.

"We have Kai," he says, as he listens to a voice in his ear.

I have him in a headlock. I've won. Just a little more pressure around his neck and he'll pass out.

"We have Kai," he repeats.

"Liar."

He chuckles. "Take the earpiece out and listen for yourself."

I do.

I listen.

And the voice says he has Kai.

"Prove it," I say.

And then I hear the most beautiful, tortured sound—Kai's breath.

It's heavy and pained.

She's alive, but barely.

But I know it's her breath.

Felix has her.

I lost.

"Make a trade. Me for her," I say with too much desperation.

Felix thinks for a moment. "Why would I want you? When I have so many more uses for Kai…"

I tighten my grip. "If you want to live, you'll make the trade."

He smirks.

"What are your terms?" he asks.

"You get me. And you release her. You don't touch her. You don't hurt her. You provide her protection. You ensure she lives a long and happy life wherever she wants. You don't let her die."

"Deal."

I release Felix.

It may not make sense to most, but I know he's a man of his word. This is what he's wanted all along—me.

He can pretend he wants Kai, like Milo did. But she isn't his target. *I am.*

Felix has hated me since I killed his brother.

Felix had a heart before me, and I obliterated it when I killed Pietro.

Kai just pushed Felix over the edge when she killed Milo.

Felix pulls his gun out and aims it at me.

I don't move.

He could easily kill me.

But that's not what he wants.

He plans on torturing me.

He doesn't realize the only thing that could truly torture me is Kai. He can do whatever he wants with my body.

"Get in the car," he says, pointing to a Range Rover.

I climb into the back seat. Felix climbs into the seat next to me, while his men get in the front.

We start driving.

And I pray Kai is okay. That she will forgive me for trading my life for her's and our son's. But she had to know this was always how our story ends. And if I am going to die, I always wanted it to be for her.

I glance in the rearview mirror as we start driving away from my house engulfed in flames—burning slowly to the ground. I don't know how many of my men survived. *Did Langston? Liesel? Clifton? Any of them?*

It doesn't matter now. I can't protect them, not anymore. All I could save was Kai.

Another explosion erupts, and my house is burning.

The beautiful beach—gone.

It's all gone.

We drive for an hour, maybe two. Time no longer matters.

"I want proof Kai is safe," I say.

"Of course," Felix says, with a smug grin.

Alarm bells go off at his gesture.

He pulls his cell phone out. "But first, I thought you might want to see how your side faired."

He hands me security footage of my house.

And the nightmare unfolds.

Langston getting shot and falling to the ground.

Liesel hitting her head with a deep gash as the car crashes into a tree.

And numerous shots of my men evaporating into nothing with each explosion.

There is a pit in my stomach. Langston and Liesel are dead. I know it as the security footage shows me my house is burning. Anyone still left lying on the ground, gasping for their last breaths, will perish. If the smoke inhalation doesn't get them, the fire will.

"I'm going to kill you for what you did."

Felix shakes his head. "That isn't what you are going to kill me for."

He swipes the phone.

And my heart is gone.

It's an image of Kai, lying face down on the ground, blood spilling out of her head. She's not breathing. Any rational person would say she's dead.

She can't be.

But I feel the emptiness.

My heart is gone—with her.

I jump out of the car. It's not the smartest move I've made, but then I've made too many mistakes to count.

I should stay and kill Felix, but if Kai is truly gone, it doesn't matter if I kill him today or tomorrow. I don't have to protect her from him, so there is no rush.

I start running back toward my house. I run a mile before I realize how idiotic it is to run. I hijack a car, and then I fly. We drove at least an hour away from my house, but I arrive in under thirty minutes.

What remains of my house is still burning, but it's mostly soot at this point. A few of my men are standing around staring, like they can't believe what happened.

"Langston?" I ask the first man I see.

He shakes his head in despair.

He didn't make it.

I run through the remains of the house. To the kitchen where the security footage showed Langston fall.

There is nothing left of my kitchen except the burned remains of my fridge and oven. *No Langston.*

I choke on my tears. He can't be gone.

I run down the road. I see the Escalade. Well, what little is left of it. Mostly tires and frame. *No Liesel.*

She's gone.

And then I see the spot on the ground. The spot where Kai was face down on the ground bleeding out.

No Kai.

She's gone.

I fall to my knees on the spot. My hands slam against the ground. There is so much soot and burned grass. The fire spread here. If her body was still here, she burned to ash too.

Tears fall. Hard, fast. Slow and unyielding.

My body shakes.

Trembles.

And then collapses.

Kai is gone.

My son—gone.

And I will be gone soon, too. I have nothing left to live for. Felix took it all. My own men killed the love of my life.

My hands dig into the ground, trying to hold onto what is left of her. I grasp the dirty ash, the remains of Kai, and then I feel it. The damn scrunchie with the little wooden heart I carved for her attached.

It's covered in her blood.

It's all I have left of her.

I failed.

Again.

But I won't fail in avenging her death.

26

KAI

I PICK UP THE PAYPHONE, and I dial Enzo's number. It's been two days. The battle is surely over.

It rings.

And rings.

And rings.

And then clicks over to his voicemail. I stay on the phone, waiting for the beep. But I don't speak. I just breathe into the phone, letting Enzo know I'm alive if he is. But I can't give him any other information. If he's dead and Felix is still alive, I don't want to give him any clues about where I am. *Felix can't find me.*

Slowly, I hang up the phone with tears in my eyes. Enzo can't be dead. *He can't be gone.*

I'm sure he was just busy cleaning up after the battle. He just didn't have his cell phone on him. *That's it.*

But I know it doesn't make any sense.

Enzo would have his phone on him every second waiting for my call.

But I can't face reality. He can't be dead.

I have to hold onto hope.

I climb into the rented Jeep and drive to a small fishing village in Alaska, about as far away from Miami as I could get. No one will find me here unless I want them to.

Enzo, please come find me.

I wipe the tears away as I drive. I have to focus on the road.

The road takes me up a curved road into the mountains. I'm afraid I got the address wrong, but then I see the house at the end of the road and pull into the drive.

I don't know why I'm here. This should be the last place I went. But it's also the last place anyone would ever think to look for me.

I park the car and step out, the beep of the car horn locking, alerting the man inside to my presence.

He stands at the door as I walk up the gravel sidewalk.

"What are you doing here?" he asks.

"I need answers. I need somewhere safe to go. And for some stupid reason, I thought my father might be able to help me," I say, with a glare.

He stands at the door, and for a moment, I don't think he's going to let me inside. But then he steps aside, holding the door open for me as I step inside the small mountain home.

My father walks into the kitchen and pours two cups of coffee. He hands one to me and then walks out onto the back porch. I follow. There are two rocking chairs looking out at the mountains.

It seems like I did my father a favor by firing him. He has a nicer home and life here than he did in Miami.

"I'm sorry for what I did to you, Kai. You have no idea how sorry. At the time, I thought I was preparing you for this life. I couldn't spend every day of your childhood abusing and torturing you like Enzo's father did, but I could prepare you once you were adult. So that's what I did," he says, and I see genuine tears in his eyes.

It should move me, but it doesn't. I'm stone. His tears mean nothing to me.

"I didn't come here for an apology," I say coldly.

He nods. "You came here for answers."

I nod.

"He's alive."

"What?" I sit up in my chair.

"Enzo's alive."

"How do you know that?"

"Clifton—he and I were friends before you fired me. He's kept me up to date. Enzo is alive."

I exhale and sob into my hands. *He's alive.*

"But that doesn't mean you are."

"What do you mean? Of course, I'm alive. I'm not a ghost," I say, not understanding.

"Enzo thinks you're dead. And I haven't corrected Clifton."

"Why not? Tell him I'm alive!"

"No."

I growl. I've been pissed at my father before, but nothing like how I feel now. "Do you understand what kind of pain Enzo must be in, thinking I'm dead? Call Clifton right now and tell him to tell Enzo I'm alive!"

"No. Felix is still alive. You are still in danger. Your child is still in danger," my father stares at the stomach I can no longer hide.

I frown and lean back. *I'm still not safe.*

Felix is alive.

"But even if Felix were dead, I still wouldn't tell Enzo you are alive."

"Why not?"

"Because the only way you get to live is to pretend you are dead."

"I don't understand."

My father takes a deep breath, with pain I've never seen on his face before. He sets his cup of coffee down on the table next to him. He stands and walks to the edge of the deck and leans on the banister.

I stand and walk over next to my father. I lean on the railing next to him. We both stare out at the wilderness behind his house. It's breathtaking, but the view isn't what is taking my breath away. My father is. I'm patient. I know whatever he is about to say is important. But it's still hard waiting.

Finally, my father looks me in the eyes with tears streaming down his face.

"I'm not your father, Kai."

"What? Yes, you are. You raised me since I was little. We look exactly alike."

He puts a hand on my shoulder, and I stop talking.

"I'm your uncle."

"I don't understand."

"Your father died, fighting to become Mr. Black."

My heart stops. "What? How?"

"The final game..."

I hold my breath, but I already know what my father, or my uncle, is about to say. I think I've always known.

Enzo has my heart. He's always possessed it. The truth is the one thing I've always wanted, but knew deep down would take away everything I love.

"The final game is always the same. It's why you have to have heirs before the game starts. Because only one will survive the final game. The final game only ends when one of you dies, and one of you lives."

I squeeze my eyes shut, trying to keep the pain in.

"Your father died at Enzo's father's hands. I was named your guardian. I raised you and did what I could to protect you. I sold you to give you strength and hoped it was enough for you to survive the final game."

More tears.

"Because I can't watch another family member die at the hand of a Rinaldi."

"Enzo won't kill me."

My father pulls me into a hug as I continue to sob. "If you go back, he won't have a choice. If Felix doesn't kill you, then you will have to fight to the death to win the empire. The men won't settle for anything less. Either one of you dies, or they will kill you both."

I nod, understanding what this means. I finally have a way to save both Enzo and my baby. Enzo will kill Felix. It may take some time, but it will eventually happen. He will rebuild the Black organization with the men and women who survived and were loyal to him. He will be named Mr. Black.

But if I go back, they will force us to continue the game.

And then one or both of us will die. But I can protect them both—Enzo and my child.

"Then, I'll stay dead." Because if I'm dead, Enzo lives. Then my child is safe. But my heart, my heart will never recover. Because dying means never seeing Enzo again.

The End

Thank you so much for reading! Enzo and Kai's story continues in Consumed by Truths #6!

Grab Consumed by Truths #6 Here!

TRUTH OR LIES SERIES:

Lured by Lies #0.5
Taken by Lies #1
Betrayed by Truths #2
Trapped by Lies #3
Stolen by Truths #4
Possessed by Lies #5
Consumed by Truths #6

FREE BOOKS

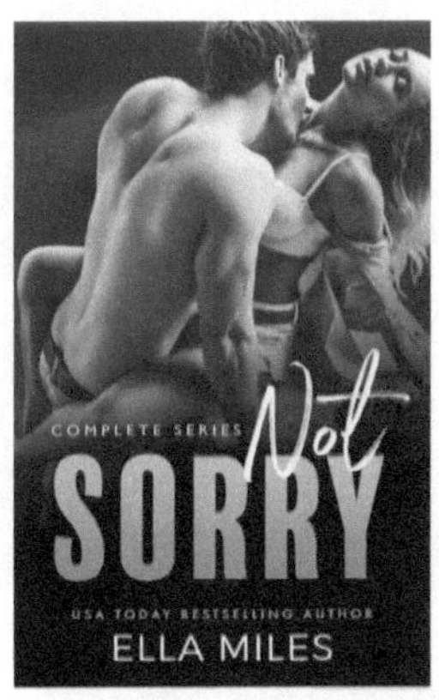

Read **Not Sorry** for **FREE!** And sign up to get my latest releases, updates, and more goodies here→EllaMiles.com/freebooks

Follow me on BookBub to get notified of my new releases and recommendations here→Follow on BookBub Here

Join Ella's Bellas FB group for giveaways and FUN & a FREE copy of **Pretend I'm Yours**→Join Ella's Bellas Here

Order Signed Paperbacks→https://ellamiles.com/signed-paperbacks

ALSO BY ELLA MILES

TRUTH OR LIES (Coming 2019):

Lured by Lies #0.5

Taken by Lies #1

Betrayed by Truths #2

Trapped by Lies #3

Stolen by Truths #4

Possessed by Lies #5

Consumed by Truths #6

DIRTY SERIES:

Dirty Beginning

Dirty Obsession

Dirty Addiction

Dirty Revenge

Dirty: The Complete Series

ALIGNED SERIES:

Aligned: Volume 1 (Free Series Starter)

Aligned: Volume 2

Aligned: Volume 3

Aligned: Volume 4

Aligned: The Complete Series Boxset

UNFORGIVABLE SERIES:

Heart of a Thief

Heart of a Liar

Heart of a Prick

Unforgivable: The Complete Series Boxset

MAYBE, DEFINITELY SERIES:

Maybe Yes

Maybe Never

Maybe Always

Definitely Yes

Definitely No

Definitely Forever

STANDALONES:

Pretend I'm Yours

Finding Perfect

Savage Love

Too Much

Not Sorry

ABOUT THE AUTHOR

Ella Miles writes steamy romance, including everything from dark suspense romance that will leave you on the edge of your seat to contemporary romance that will leave you laughing out loud or crying. Most importantly, she wants you to feel everything her characters feel as you read.

Ella is currently living her own happily ever after near the Rocky Mountains with her high school sweetheart husband. Her heart is also taken by her goofy five year old black lab who is scared of everything, including her own shadow.

Ella is a USA Today Bestselling Author & Top 50 Bestselling Author.

Stalk Ella at:
www.ellamiles.com
ella@ellamiles.com